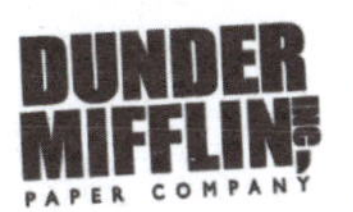

Week of:

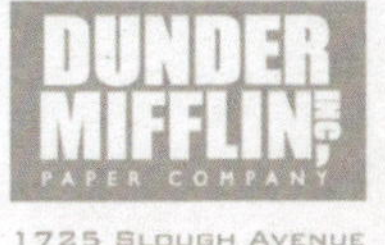

1725 Slough Avenue
Scranton, PA 18505

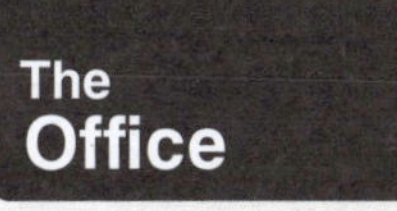

WEEKLY PLAN

NOTES

MONDAY	TUESDAY
WEDNESDAY	THURSDAY
FRIDAY	SATURDAY
	SUNDAY

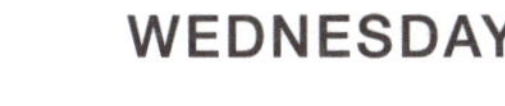

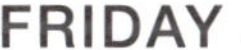

TOP PRIORITIES

BEFORE I DO ANYTHING I ASK MYSELF, 'WOULD AN IDIOT DO THAT?' AND IF THE ANSWER IS YES, I DO NOT DO THAT THING.

THINGS TO DO

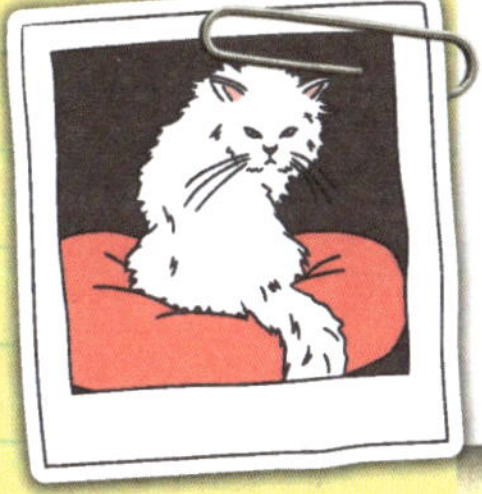

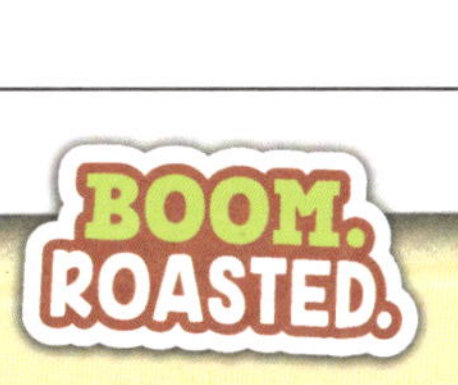

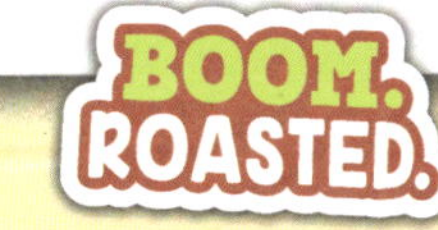

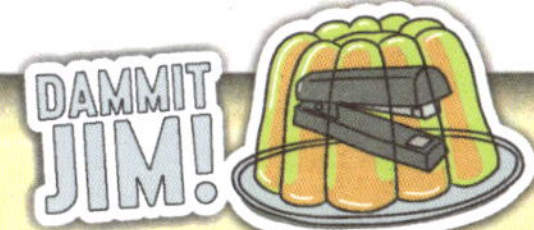

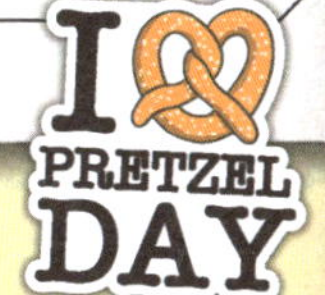

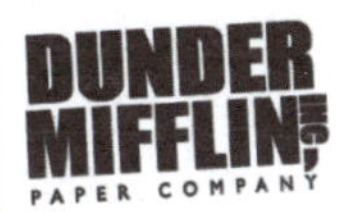

Week of:

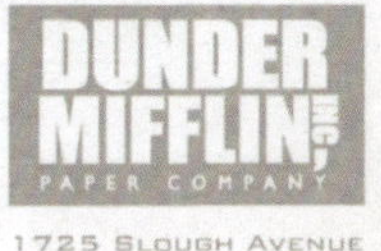

1725 Slough Avenue
Scranton, PA 18505

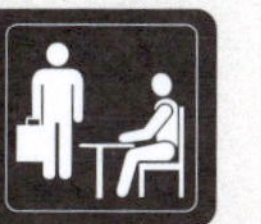

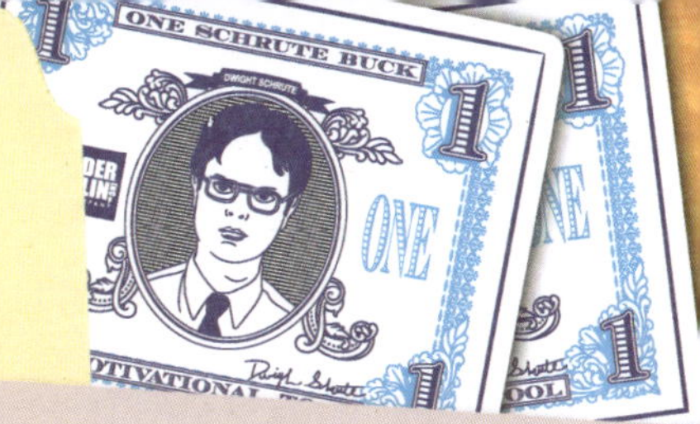

WEEKLY PLAN

NOTES

MONDAY	TUESDAY
WEDNESDAY	THURSDAY
FRIDAY	SATURDAY
	SUNDAY

DUNDIE AWARD

TOP PRIORITIES

BEFORE I DO ANYTHING I ASK MYSELF, 'WOULD AN IDIOT DO THAT?' AND IF THE ANSWER IS YES, I DO NOT DO THAT THING.

THINGS TO DO

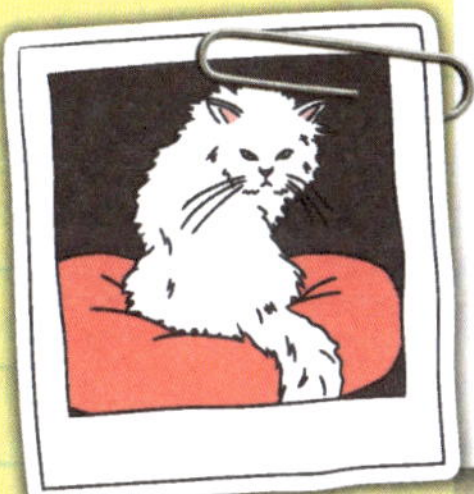

WORLD'S BEST BOSS

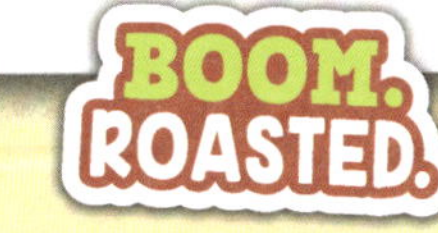

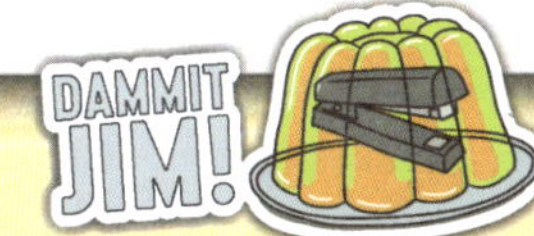

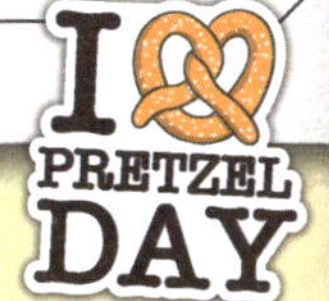

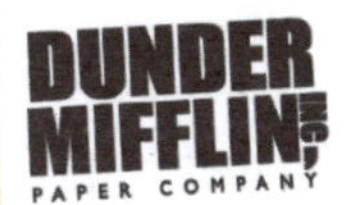

Week of: ______

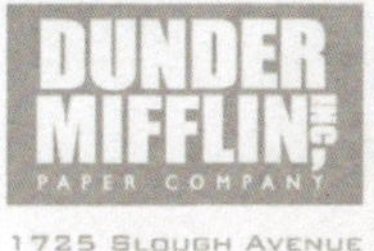

1725 Slough Avenue
Scranton, PA 18505

The Office 

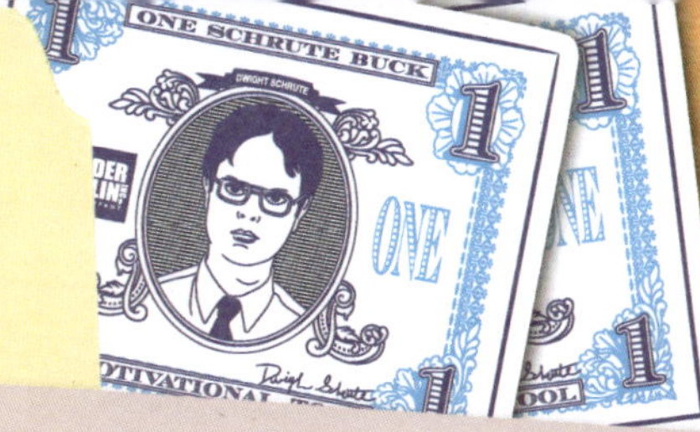

WEEKLY PLAN

NOTES

MONDAY	TUESDAY
WEDNESDAY	THURSDAY
FRIDAY	SATURDAY SUNDAY

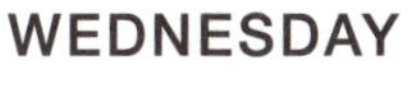

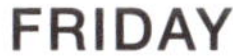

TOP PRIORITIES

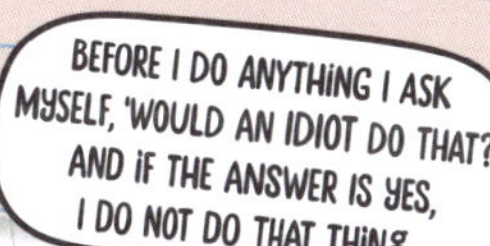

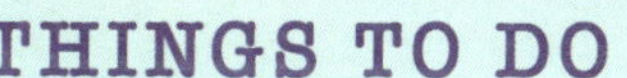

THINGS TO DO

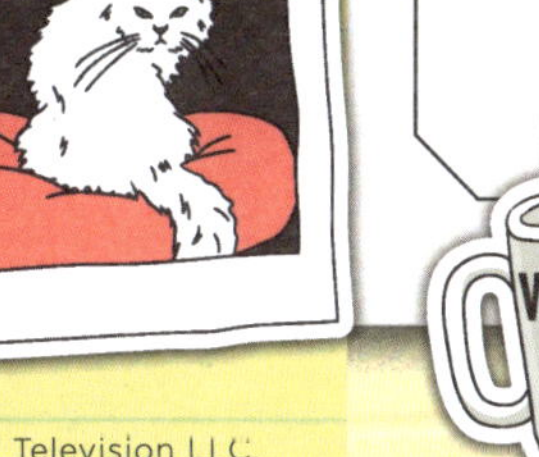

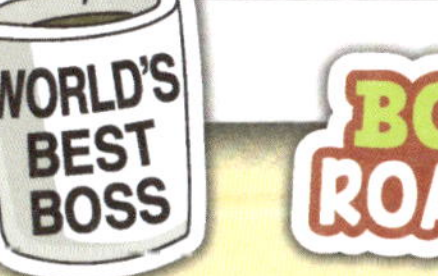

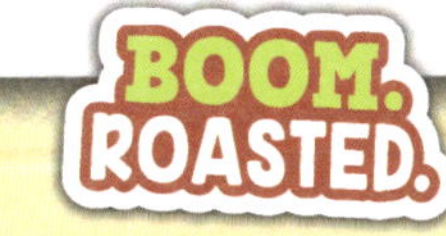

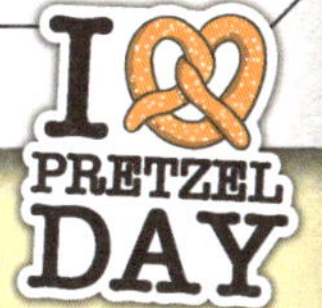

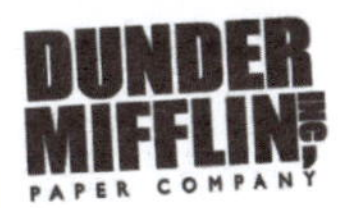

Week of:

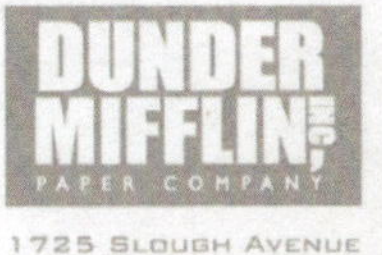

1725 Slough Avenue
Scranton, PA 18505

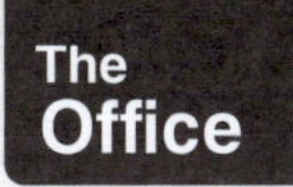

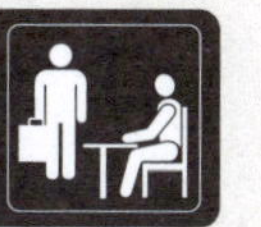

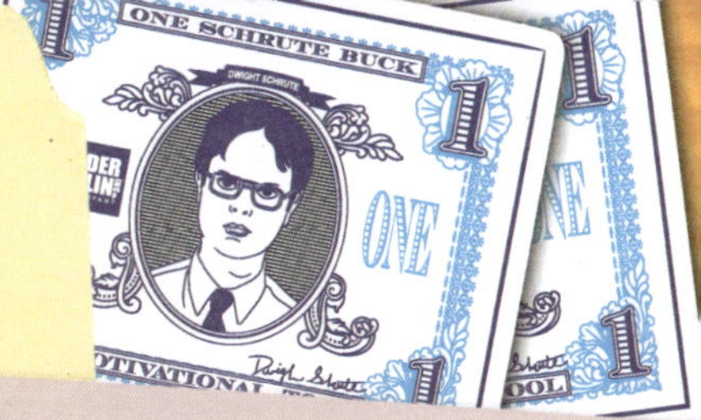

WEEKLY PLAN

NOTES

MONDAY	TUESDAY
WEDNESDAY	THURSDAY
FRIDAY	SATURDAY
	SUNDAY

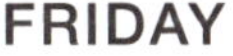

TOP PRIORITIES

BEFORE I DO ANYTHING I ASK MYSELF, 'WOULD AN IDIOT DO THAT?' AND IF THE ANSWER IS YES, I DO NOT DO THAT THING.

THINGS TO DO

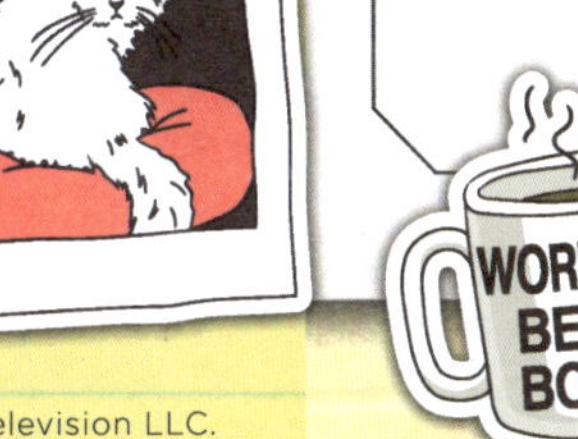

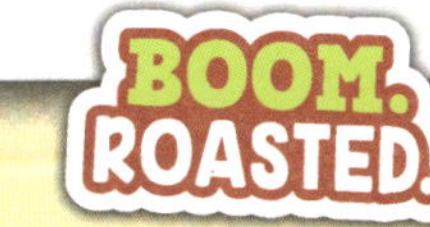

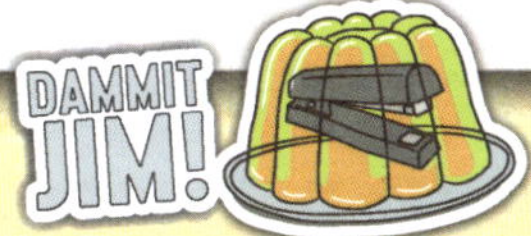

DAMMIT JIM!

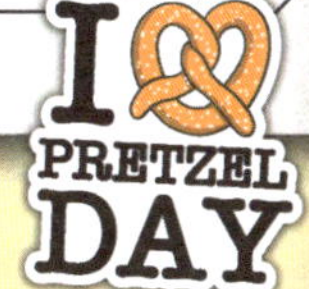

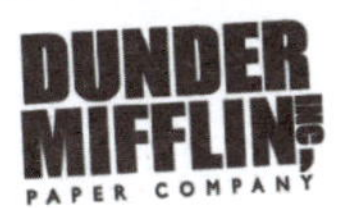

Week of:

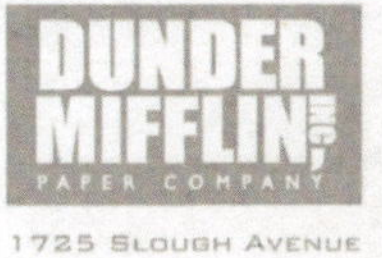

1725 Slough Avenue
Scranton, PA 18505

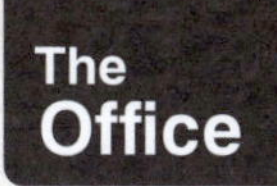
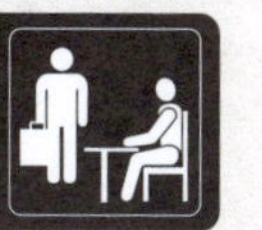

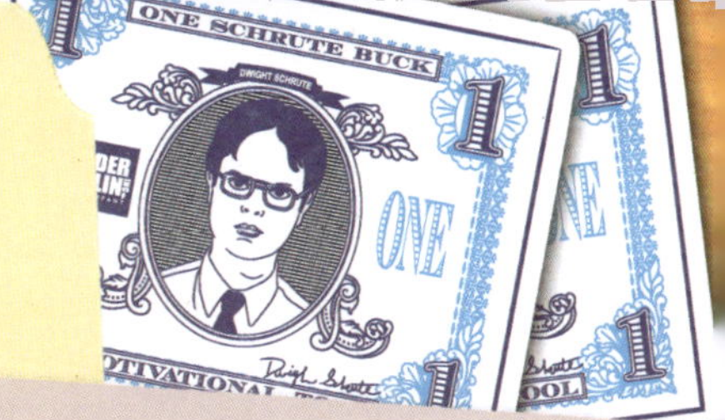

WEEKLY PLAN

NOTES

MONDAY	TUESDAY

WEDNESDAY	THURSDAY

FRIDAY	SATURDAY
	SUNDAY

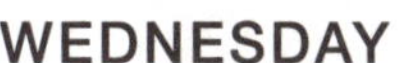
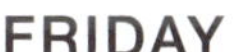

TOP PRIORITIES

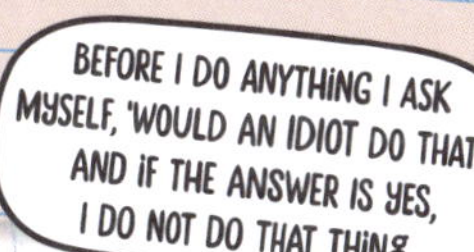
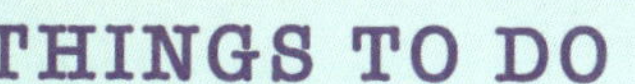

THINGS TO DO

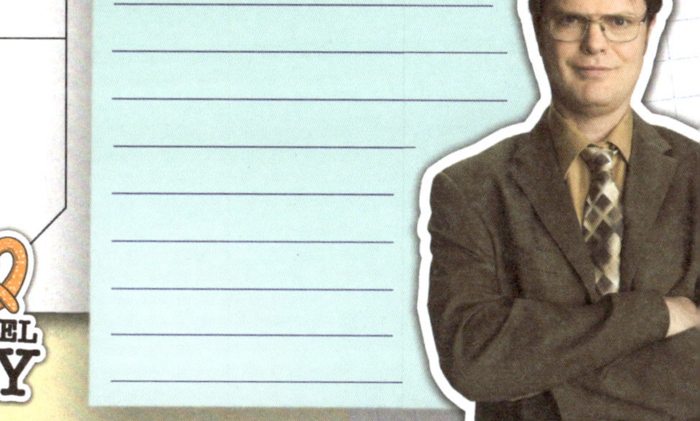

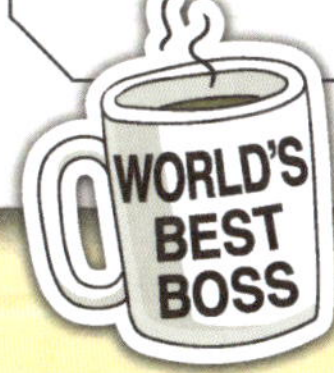

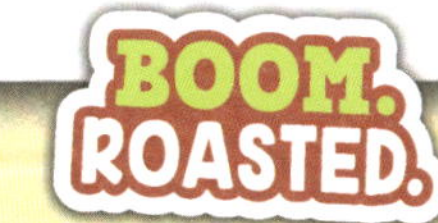

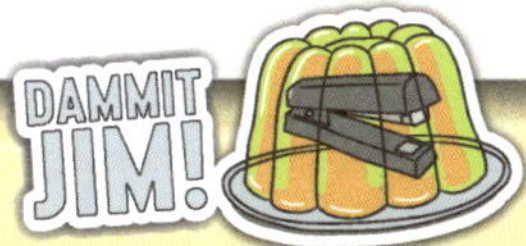

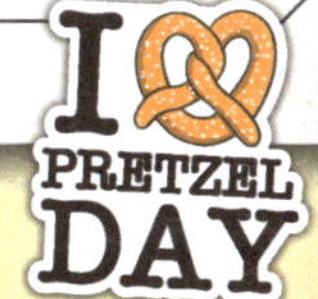

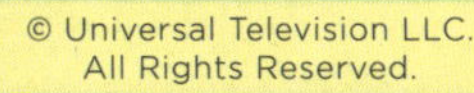

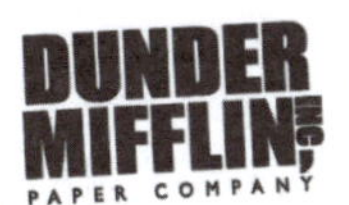

Week of:

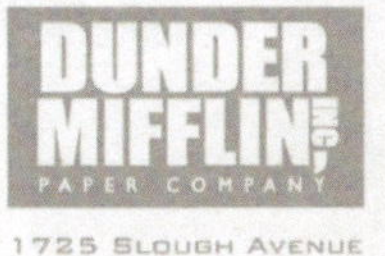

1725 Slough Avenue
Scranton, PA 18505

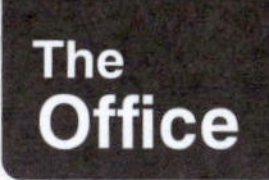

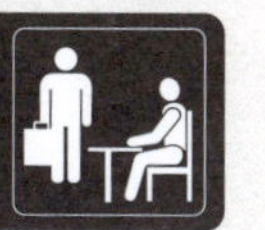

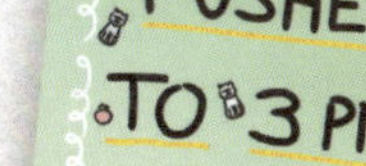

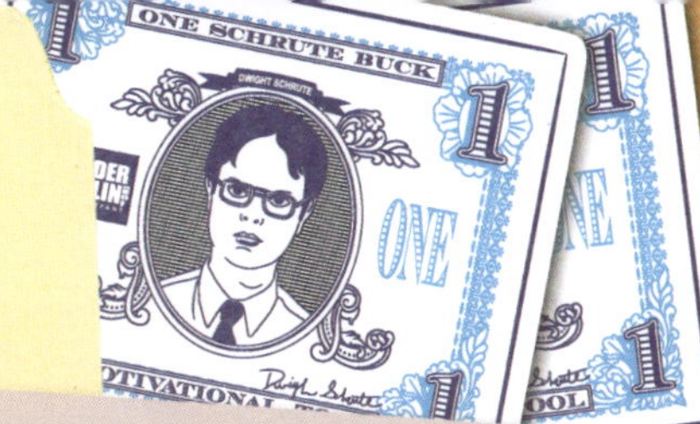

WEEKLY PLAN

NOTES

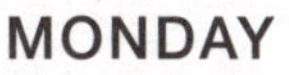

MONDAY

TUESDAY

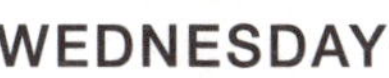

WEDNESDAY

THURSDAY

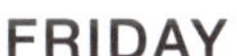

FRIDAY

SATURDAY

SUNDAY

TOP PRIORITIES

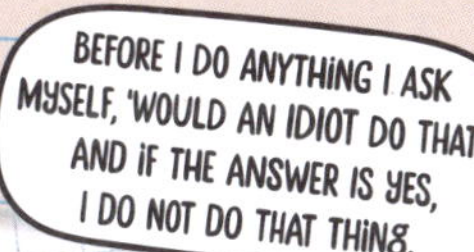

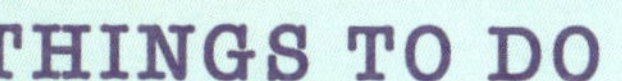

THINGS TO DO

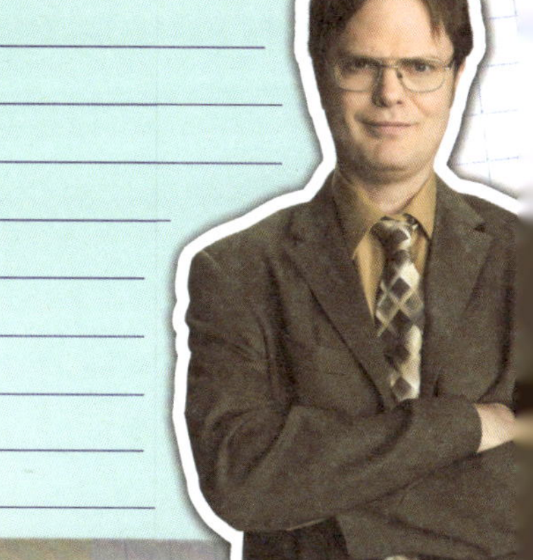

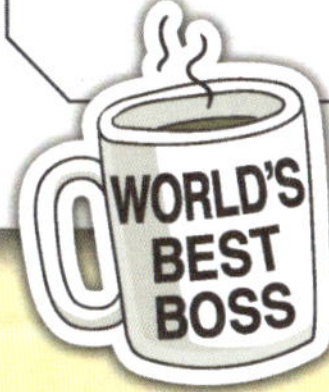

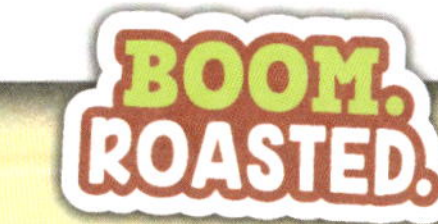

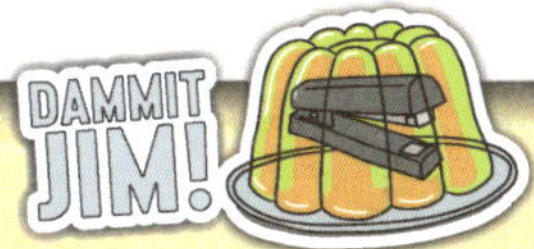

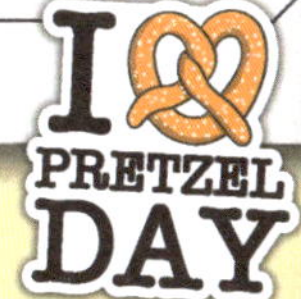

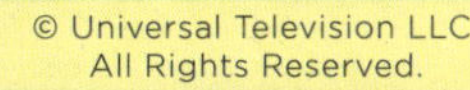

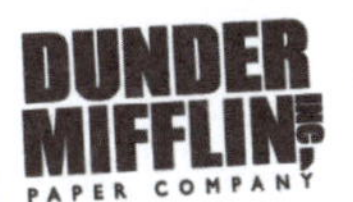

Week of:

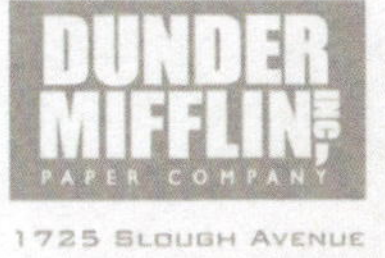

1725 Slough Avenue
Scranton, PA 18505

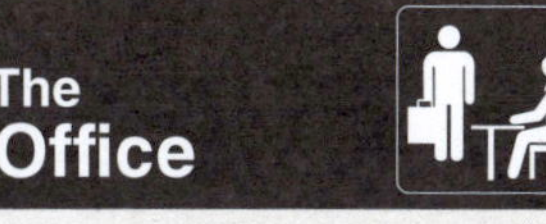

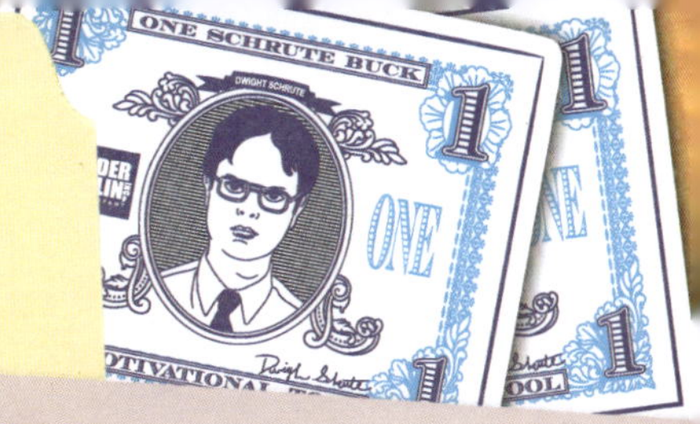

WEEKLY PLAN

NOTES

TOP PRIORITIES

MONDAY	TUESDAY
WEDNESDAY	THURSDAY
FRIDAY	SATURDAY
	SUNDAY

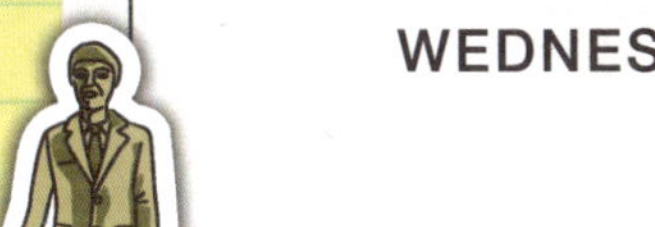

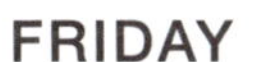

BEFORE I DO ANYTHING I ASK MYSELF, 'WOULD AN IDIOT DO THAT?' AND IF THE ANSWER IS YES, I DO NOT DO THAT THING.

THINGS TO DO

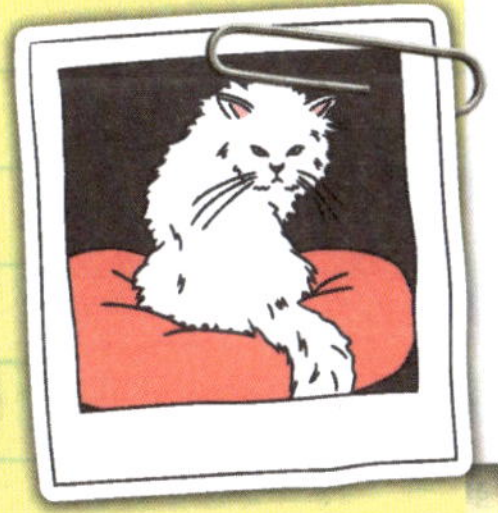

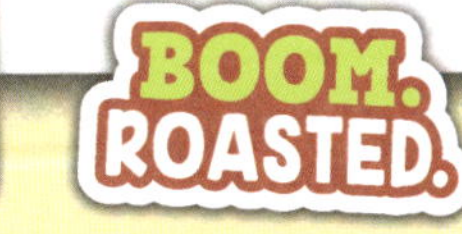

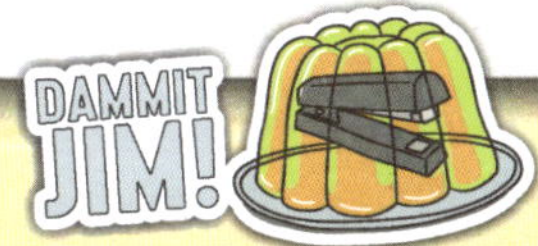

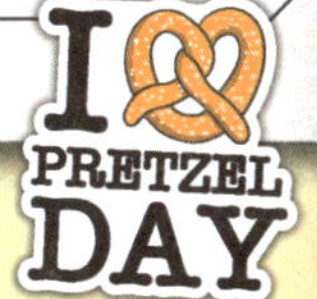

WORLD'S BEST BOSS

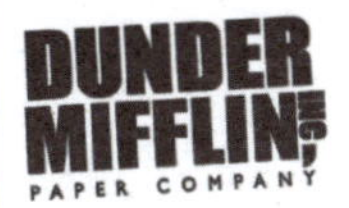

Week of:

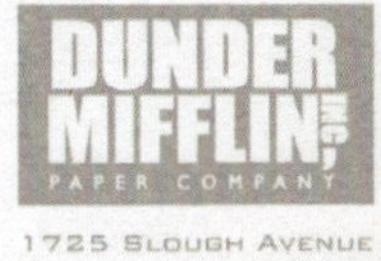

1725 Slough Avenue
Scranton, PA 18505

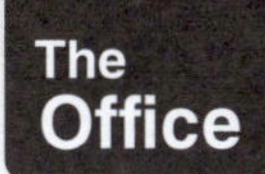

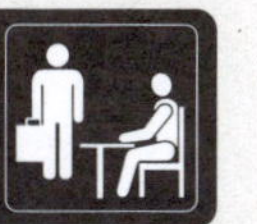

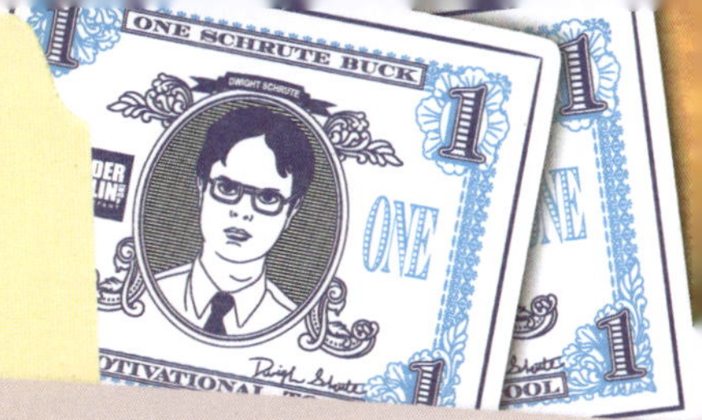

WEEKLY PLAN

NOTES

MONDAY	TUESDAY
WEDNESDAY	THURSDAY
FRIDAY	SATURDAY
	SUNDAY

TOP PRIORITIES

BEFORE I DO ANYTHING I ASK MYSELF, 'WOULD AN IDIOT DO THAT?' AND IF THE ANSWER IS YES, I DO NOT DO THAT THING.

THINGS TO DO

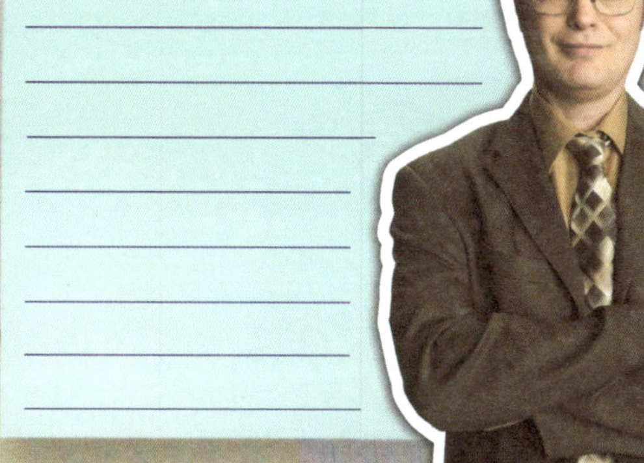

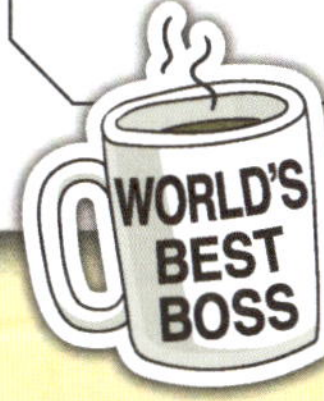

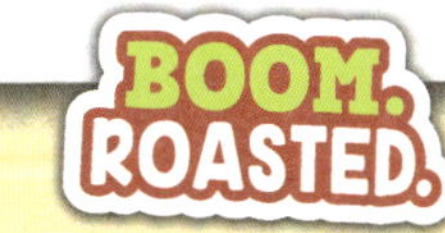

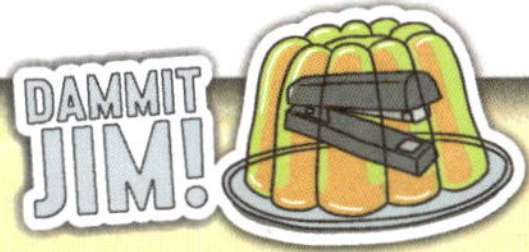

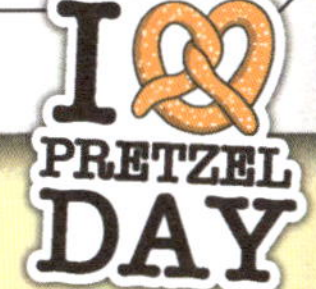

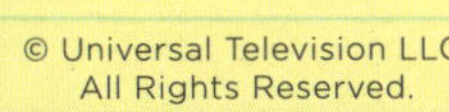

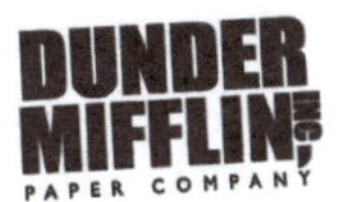

Week of:

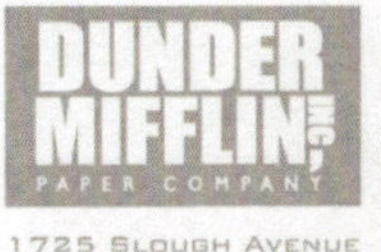

1725 Slough Avenue
Scranton, PA 18505

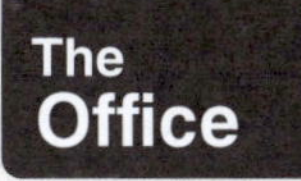

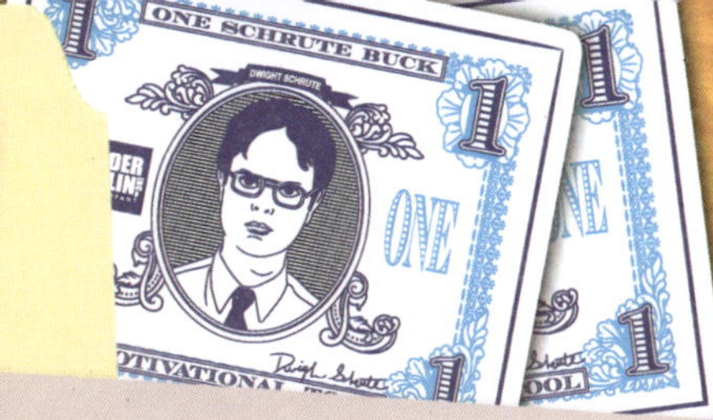

WEEKLY PLAN

NOTES

MONDAY	TUESDAY
WEDNESDAY	THURSDAY
FRIDAY	SATURDAY
	SUNDAY

TOP PRIORITIES

BEFORE I DO ANYTHING I ASK MYSELF, 'WOULD AN IDIOT DO THAT?' AND IF THE ANSWER IS YES, I DO NOT DO THAT THING.

DUNDIE AWARD

THINGS TO DO

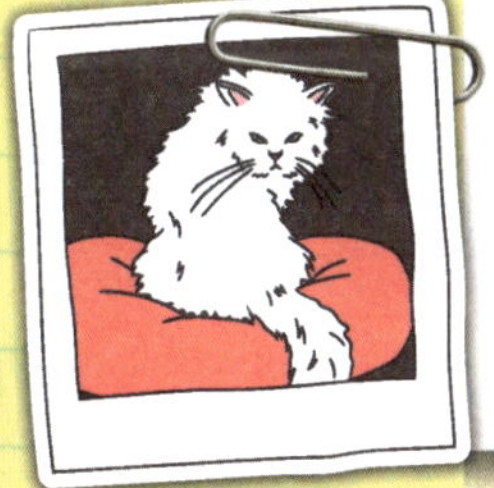

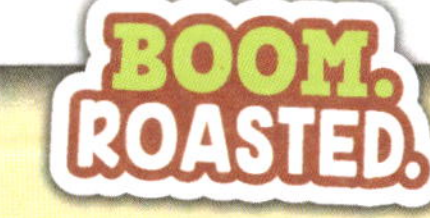

BOOM.
ROASTED.

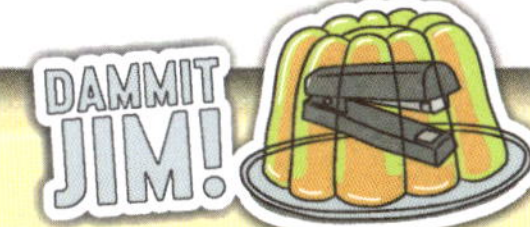

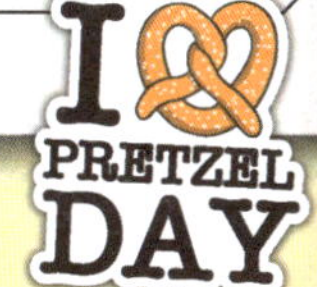

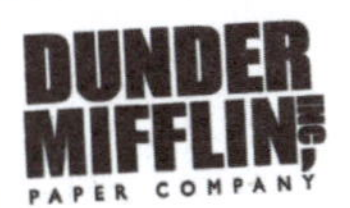

Week of:

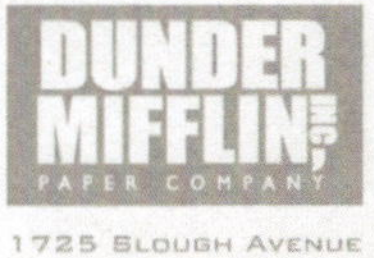

1725 Slough Avenue
Scranton, PA 18505

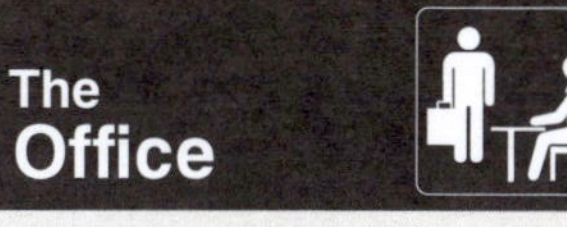

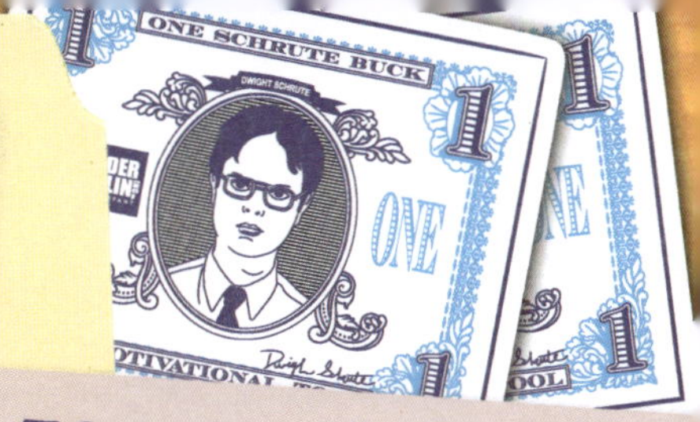

WEEKLY PLAN

NOTES

MONDAY	TUESDAY
WEDNESDAY	THURSDAY
FRIDAY	SATURDAY
	SUNDAY

DUNDIE AWARD

TOP PRIORITIES

BEFORE I DO ANYTHING I ASK MYSELF, 'WOULD AN IDIOT DO THAT?' AND IF THE ANSWER IS YES, I DO NOT DO THAT THING.

THINGS TO DO

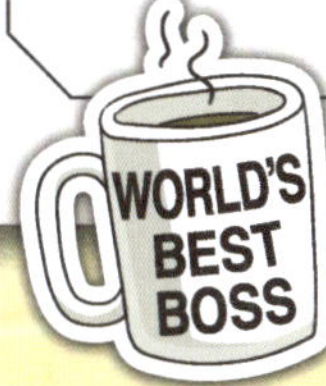

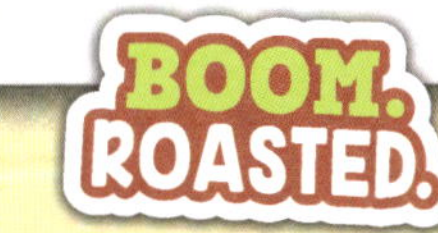

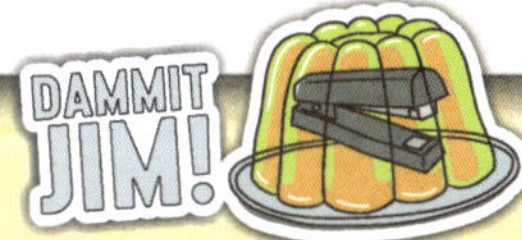

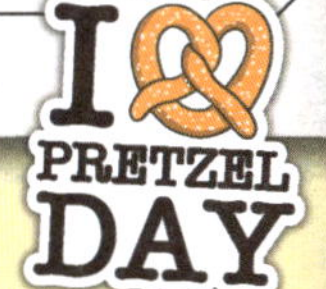

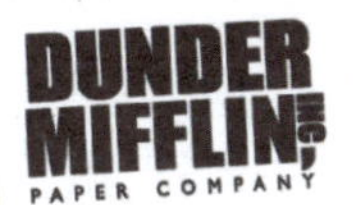

Week of:

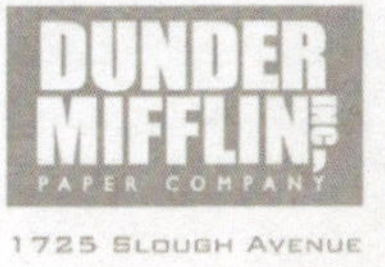

1725 Slough Avenue
Scranton, PA 18505

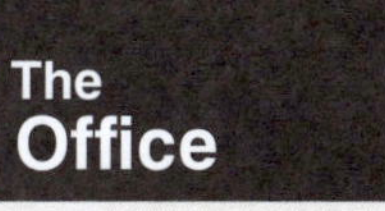

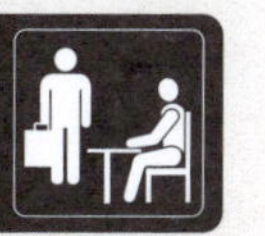

WEEKLY PLAN

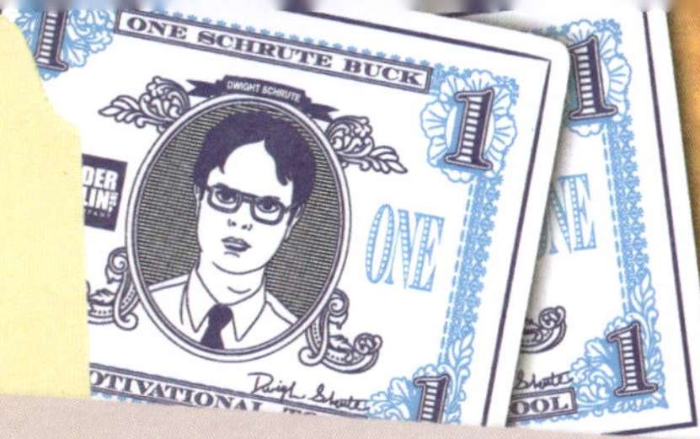

NOTES

TOP PRIORITIES

MONDAY	TUESDAY
WEDNESDAY	THURSDAY
FRIDAY	SATURDAY
	SUNDAY

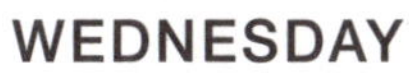

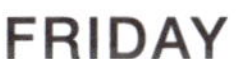

BEFORE I DO ANYTHING I ASK MYSELF, 'WOULD AN IDIOT DO THAT?' AND IF THE ANSWER IS YES, I DO NOT DO THAT THING.

THINGS TO DO

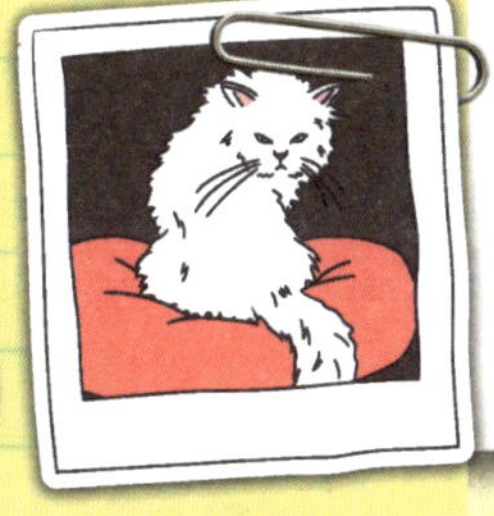

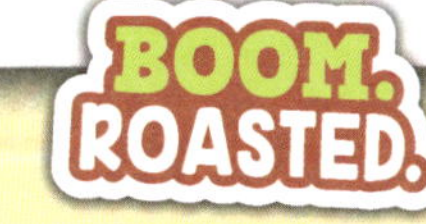

BOOM. ROASTED.

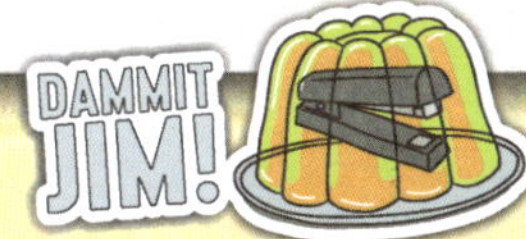

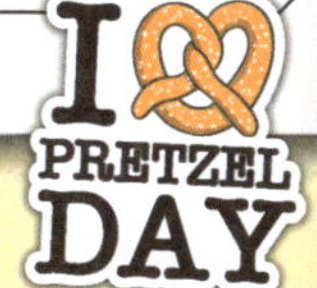

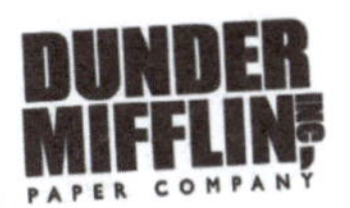

Week of:

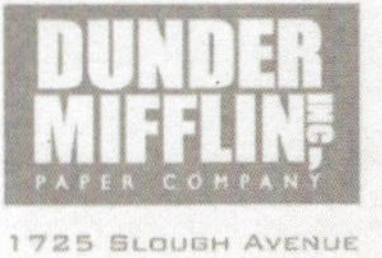

1725 Slough Avenue
Scranton, PA 18505

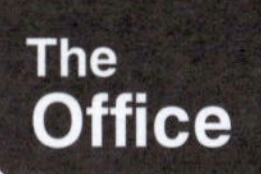

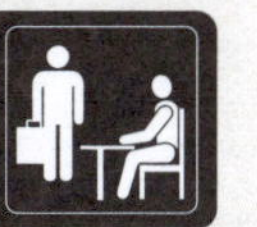

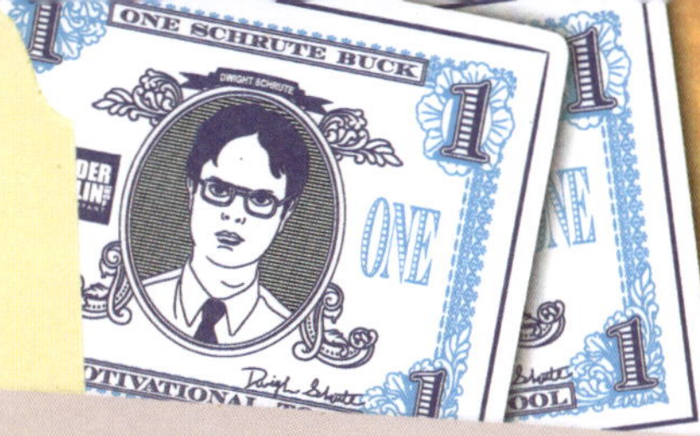

WEEKLY PLAN

NOTES

MONDAY	TUESDAY
WEDNESDAY	THURSDAY
FRIDAY	SATURDAY SUNDAY

TOP PRIORITIES

BEFORE I DO ANYTHING I ASK MYSELF, 'WOULD AN IDIOT DO THAT?' AND IF THE ANSWER IS YES, I DO NOT DO THAT THING.

DUNDIE AWARD

THINGS TO DO

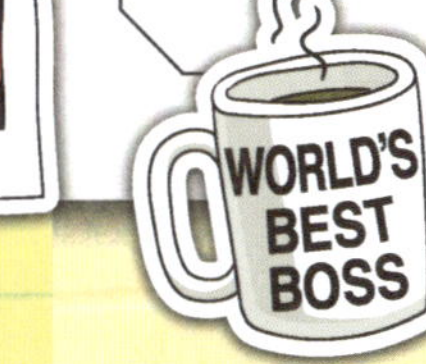

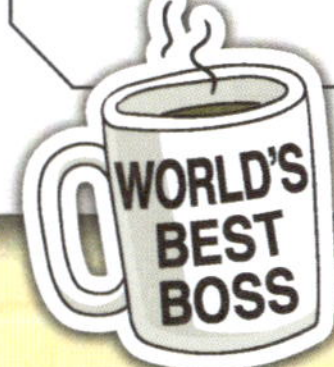

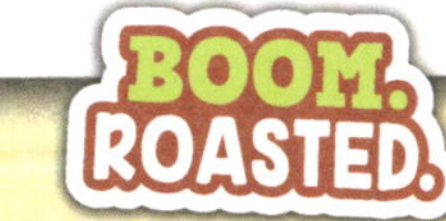

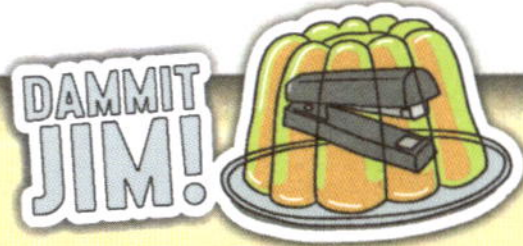

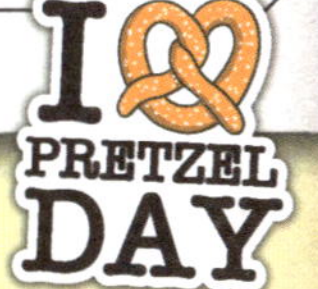

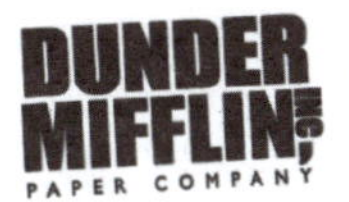

Week of:

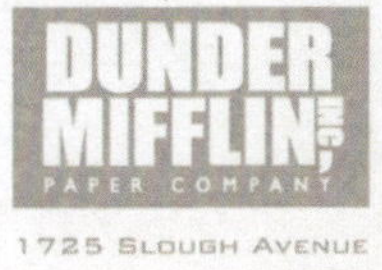

1725 Slough Avenue
Scranton, PA 18505

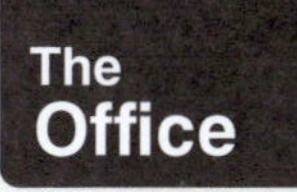

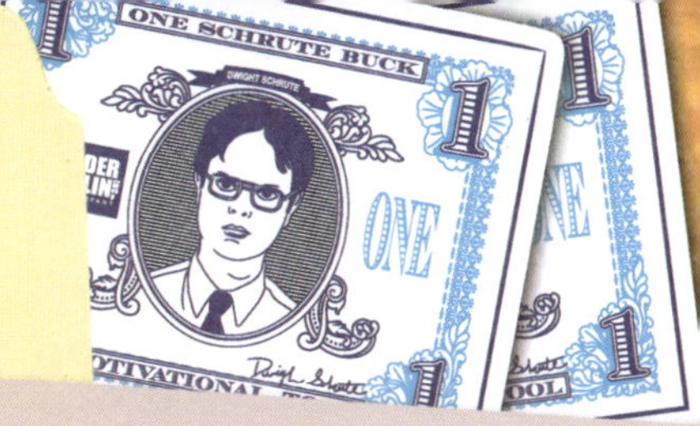

WEEKLY PLAN

NOTES

MONDAY	TUESDAY
WEDNESDAY	**THURSDAY**
FRIDAY	**SATURDAY**
	SUNDAY

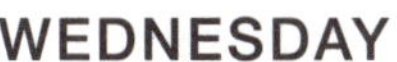

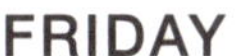

TOP PRIORITIES

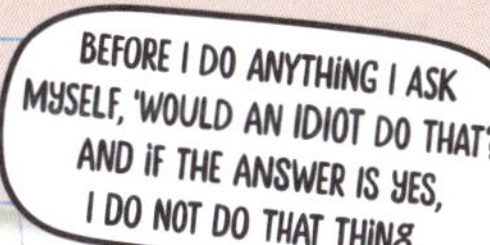

BEFORE I DO ANYTHING I ASK MYSELF, 'WOULD AN IDIOT DO THAT?' AND IF THE ANSWER IS YES, I DO NOT DO THAT THING.

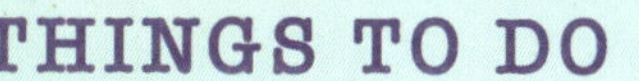

THINGS TO DO

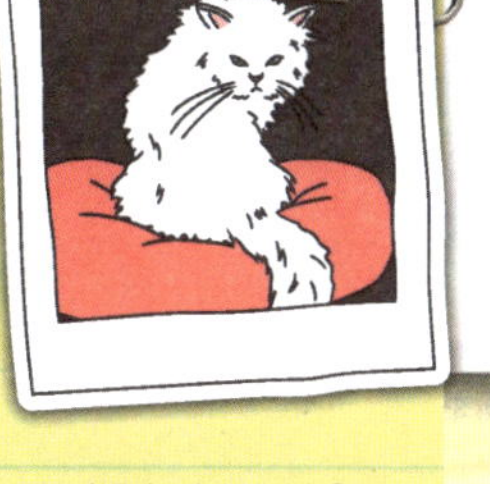

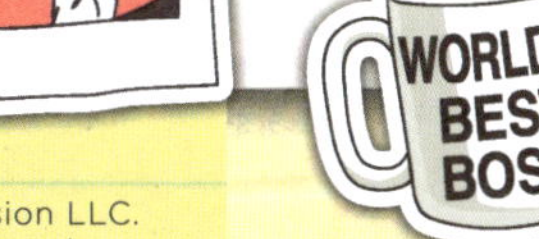

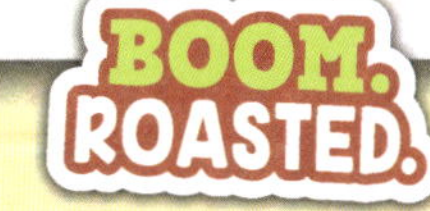

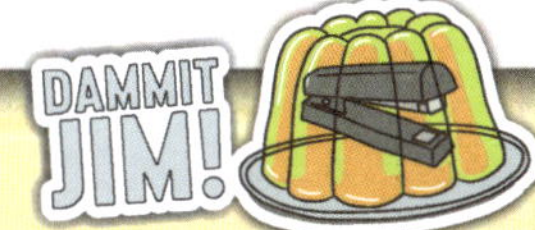

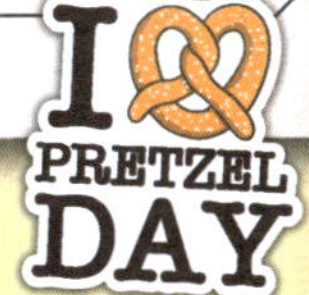

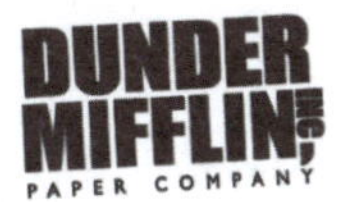

Week of:

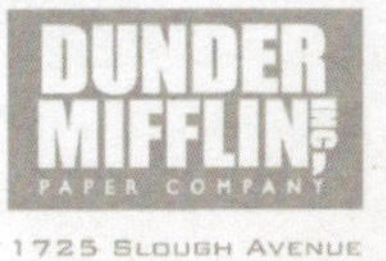

1725 Slough Avenue
Scranton, PA 18505

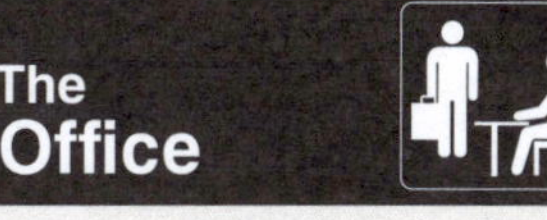

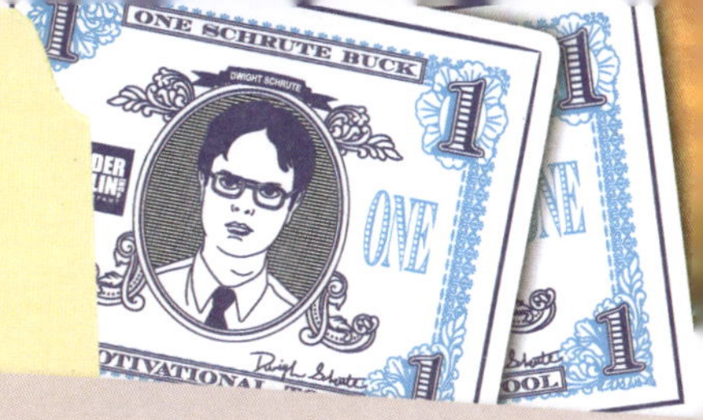

WEEKLY PLAN

MONDAY	TUESDAY
WEDNESDAY	THURSDAY
FRIDAY	SATURDAY
	SUNDAY

NOTES

TOP PRIORITIES

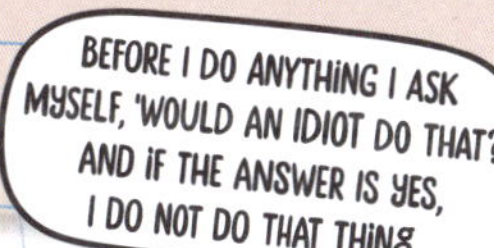

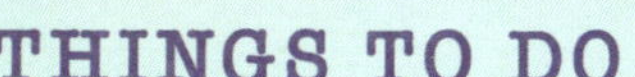

THINGS TO DO

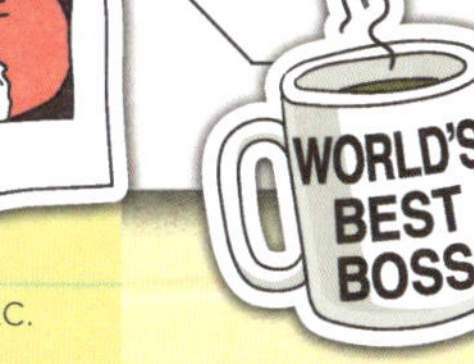

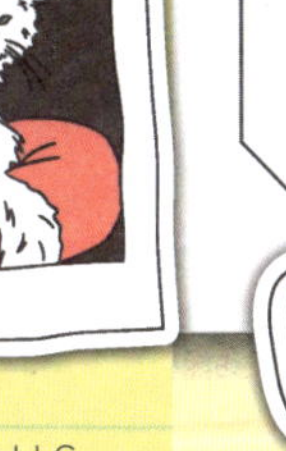

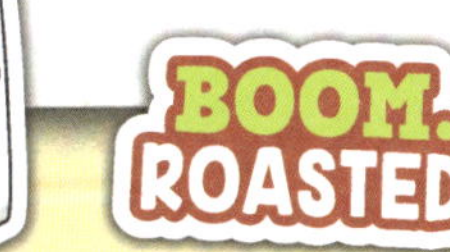

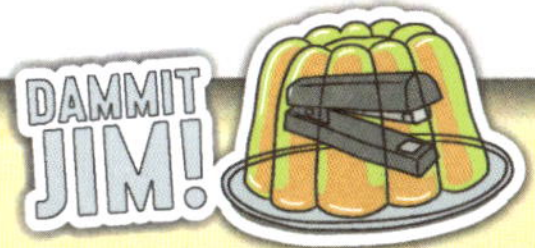

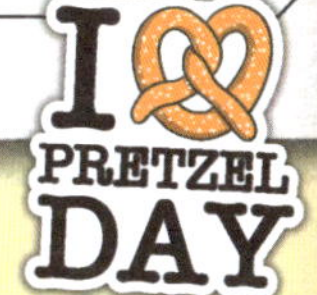

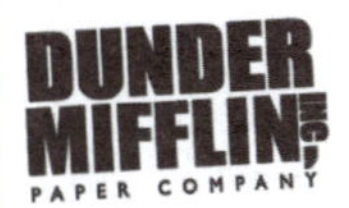

Week of:

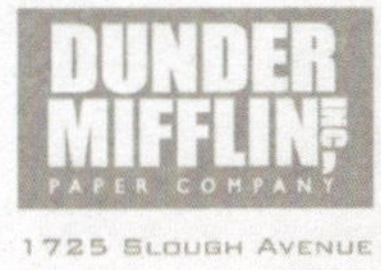

1725 Slough Avenue
Scranton, PA 18505

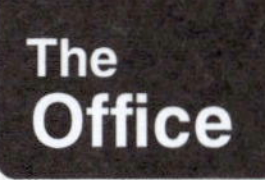

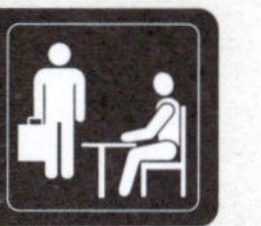

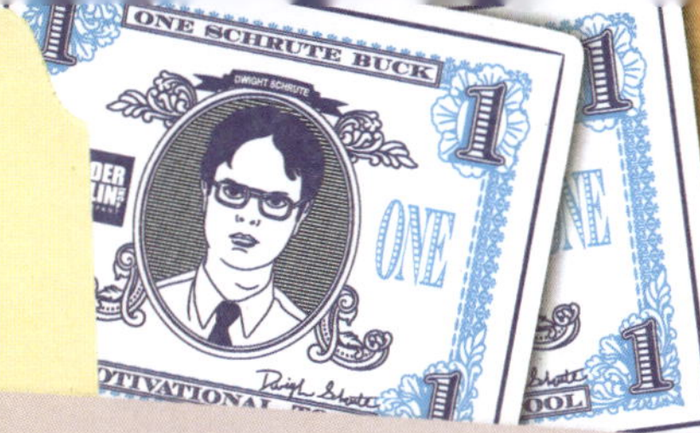

WEEKLY PLAN

NOTES

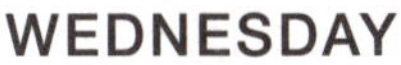

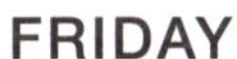

MONDAY	TUESDAY
WEDNESDAY	THURSDAY
FRIDAY	SATURDAY SUNDAY

TOP PRIORITIES

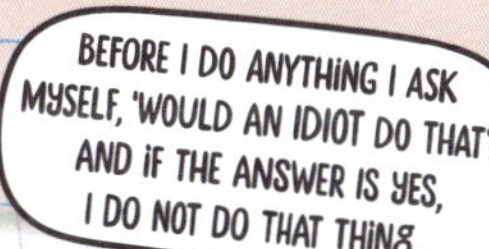

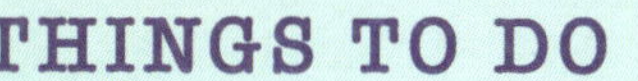

THINGS TO DO

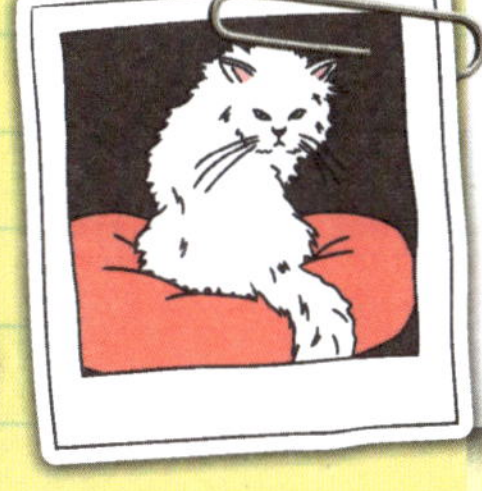

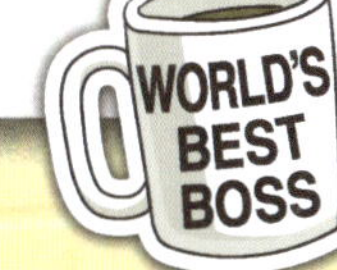

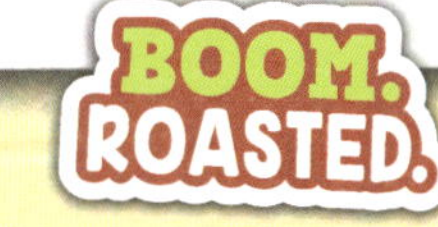

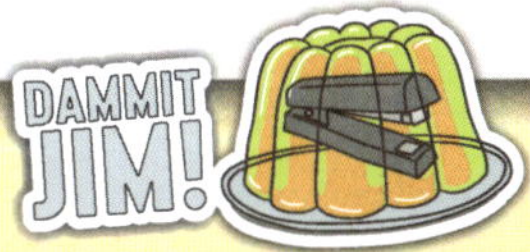

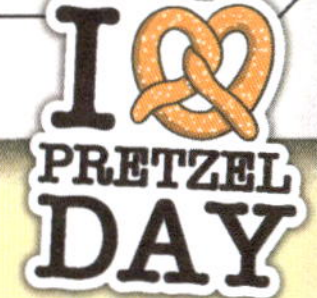

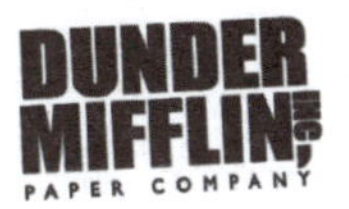

Week of:

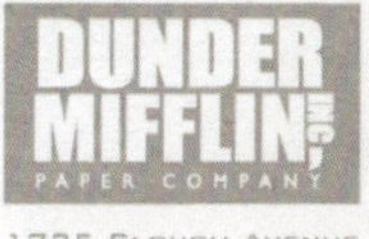

1725 Slough Avenue
Scranton, PA 18505

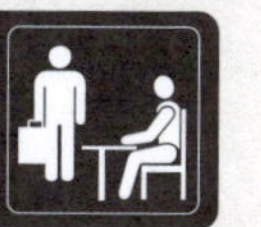

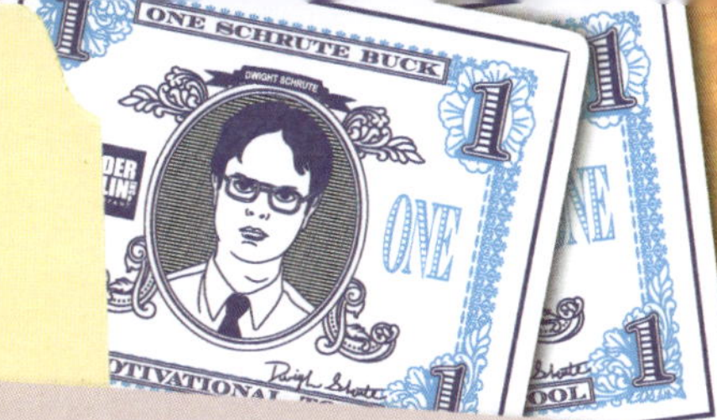

WEEKLY PLAN

NOTES

MONDAY	TUESDAY
WEDNESDAY	THURSDAY
FRIDAY	SATURDAY
	SUNDAY

TOP PRIORITIES

BEFORE I DO ANYTHING I ASK MYSELF, 'WOULD AN IDIOT DO THAT?' AND IF THE ANSWER IS YES, I DO NOT DO THAT THING.

DUNDIE AWARD

THINGS TO DO

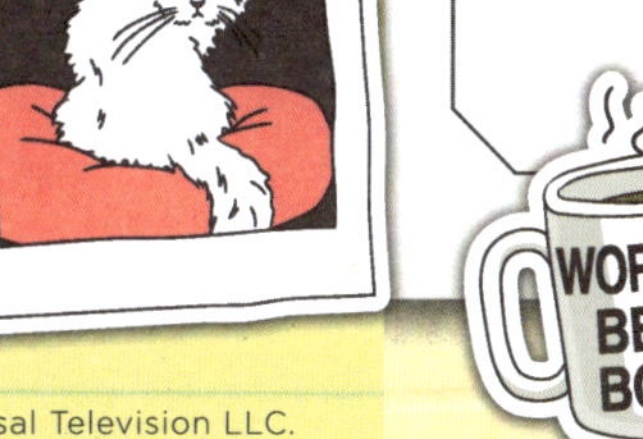

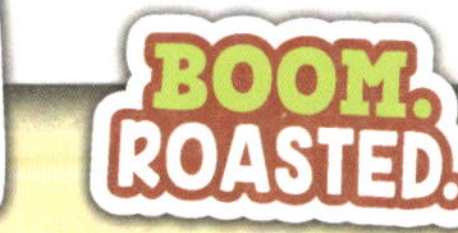

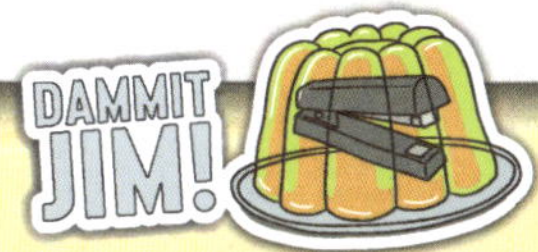

DAMMIT JIM!

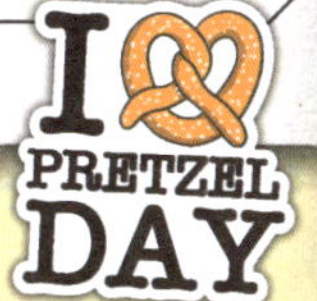

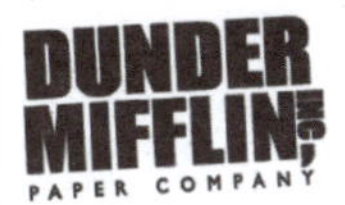

Week of:

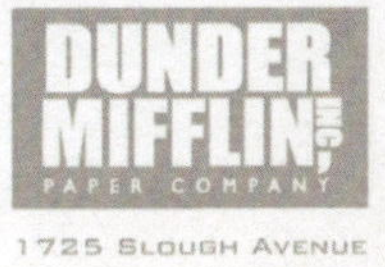

1725 Slough Avenue
Scranton, PA 18505

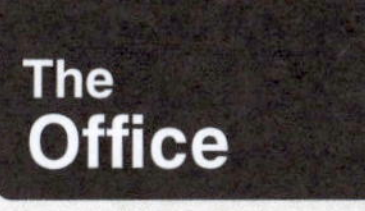

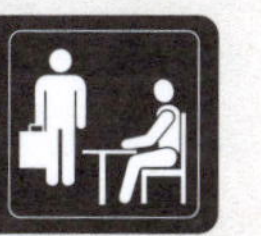

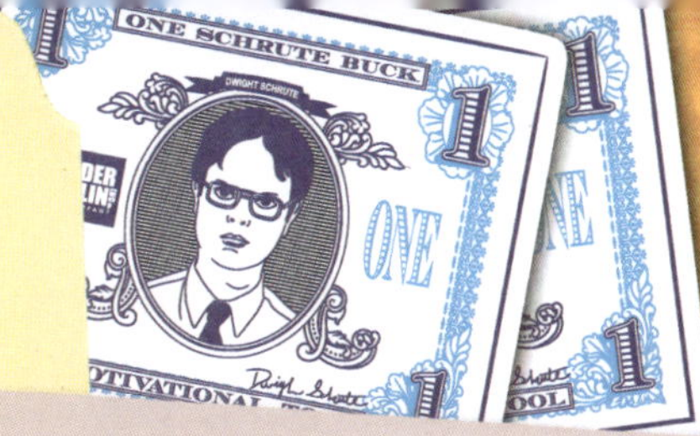

WEEKLY PLAN

NOTES

MONDAY	TUESDAY
WEDNESDAY	THURSDAY
FRIDAY	SATURDAY
	SUNDAY

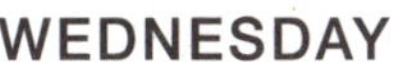

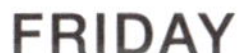

TOP PRIORITIES

BEFORE I DO ANYTHING I ASK MYSELF, 'WOULD AN IDIOT DO THAT?' AND IF THE ANSWER IS YES, I DO NOT DO THAT THING.

THINGS TO DO

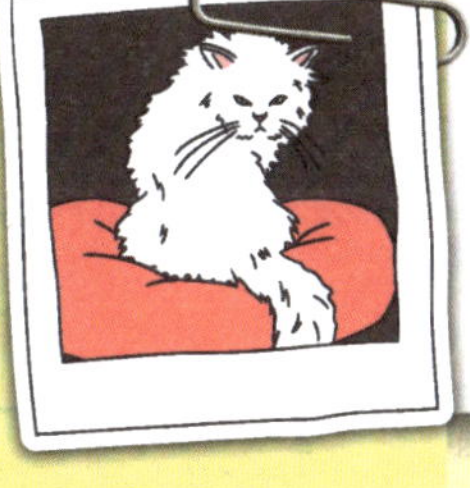

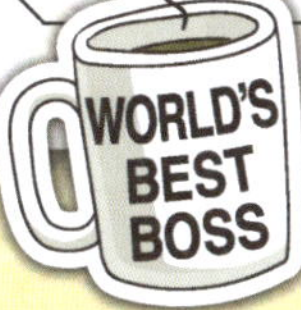

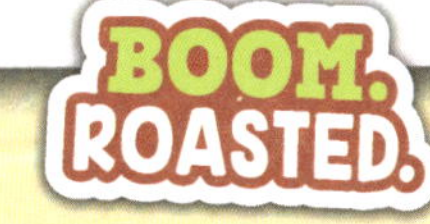

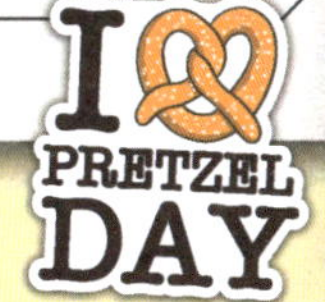

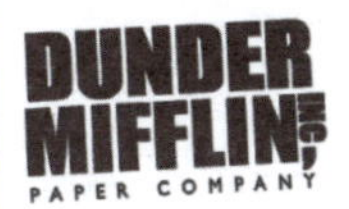

Week of:

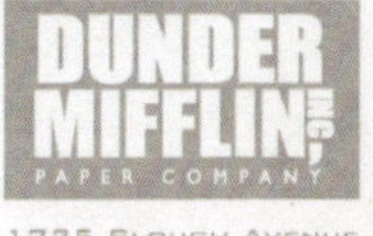

1725 Slough Avenue
Scranton, PA 18505

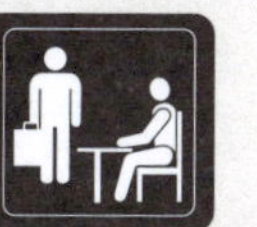

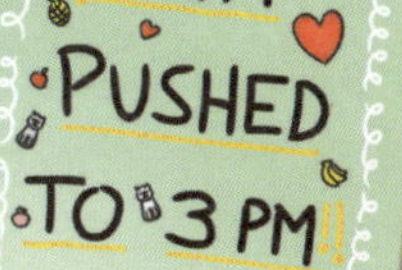

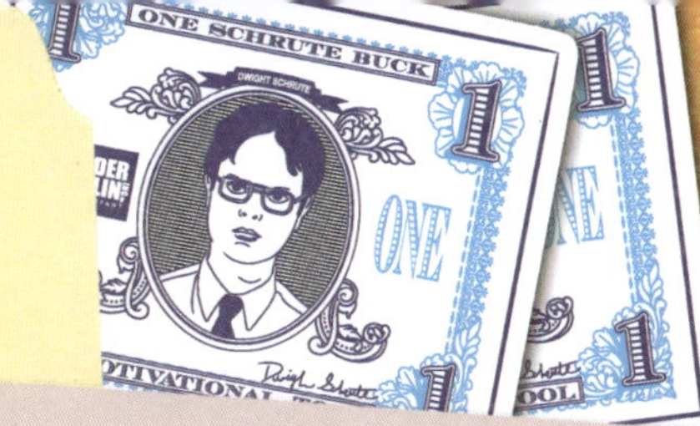

WEEKLY PLAN

NOTES

MONDAY	TUESDAY
WEDNESDAY	THURSDAY
FRIDAY	SATURDAY
	SUNDAY

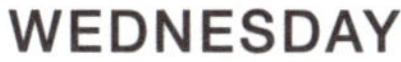

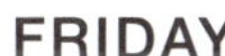

TOP PRIORITIES

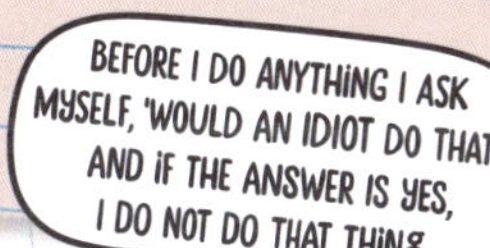

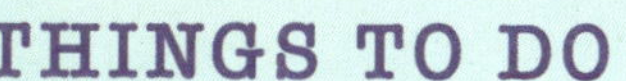

BEFORE I DO ANYTHING I ASK MYSELF, 'WOULD AN IDIOT DO THAT?' AND IF THE ANSWER IS YES, I DO NOT DO THAT THING.

THINGS TO DO

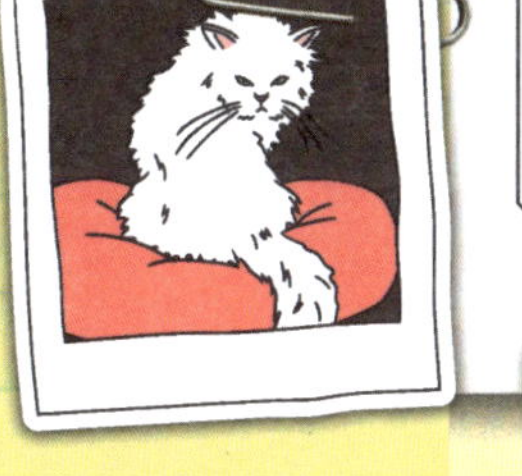

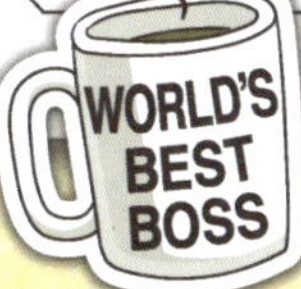

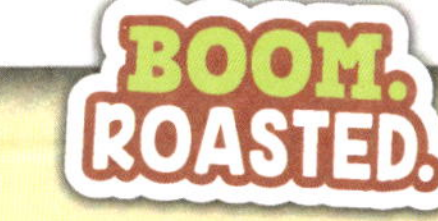

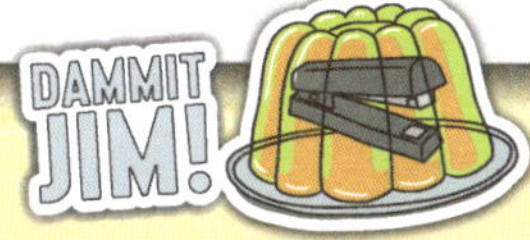

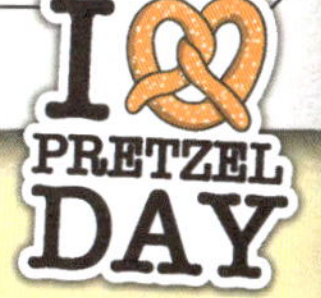

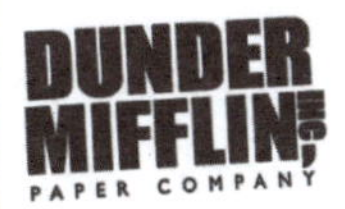

Week of:

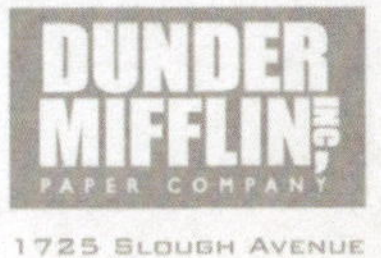

1725 Slough Avenue
Scranton, PA 18505

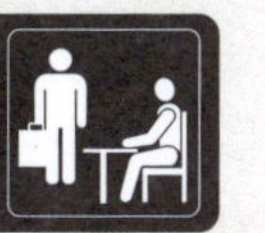

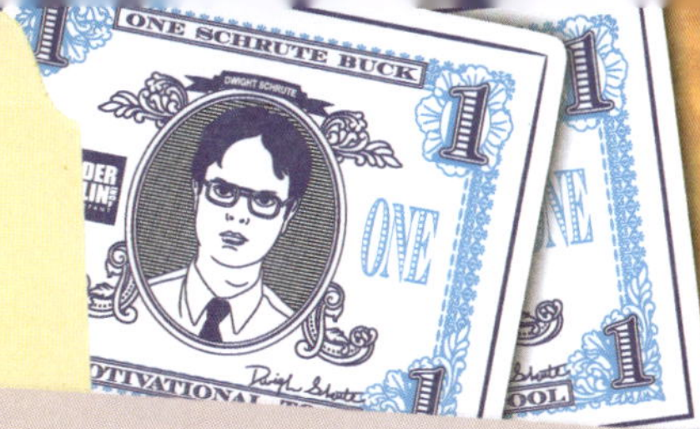

WEEKLY PLAN

NOTES

MONDAY	TUESDAY
WEDNESDAY	THURSDAY
FRIDAY	SATURDAY
	SUNDAY

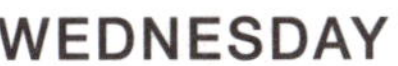
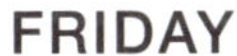

TOP PRIORITIES

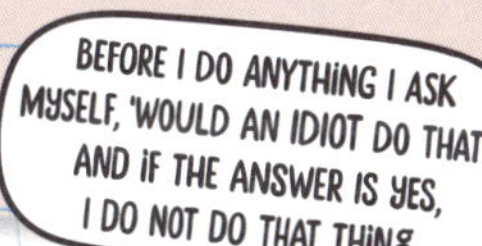

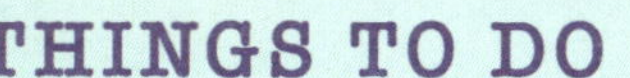

THINGS TO DO

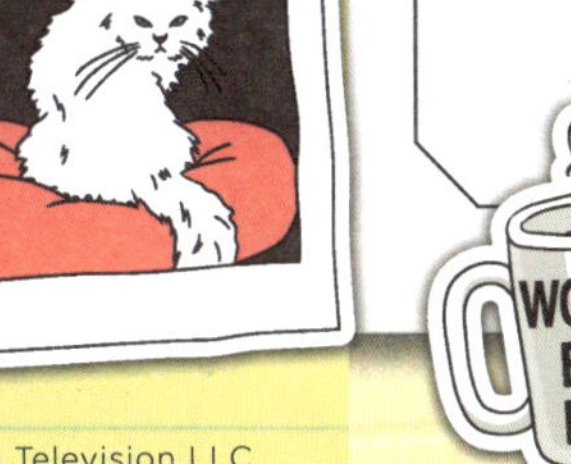
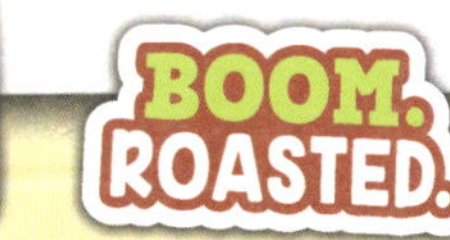

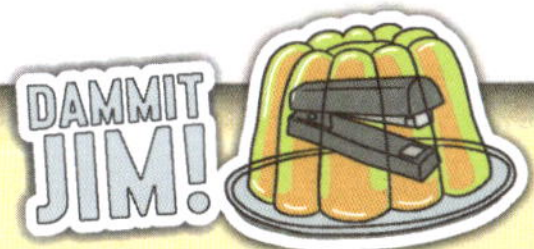

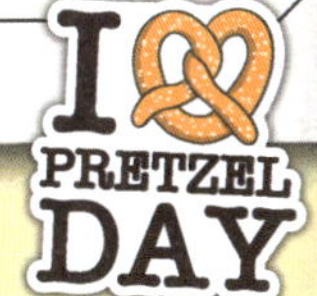

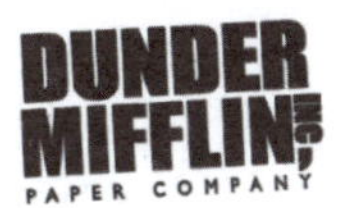

Week of:

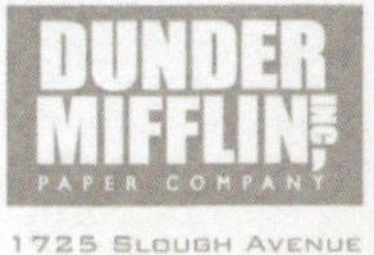

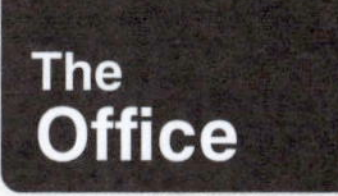

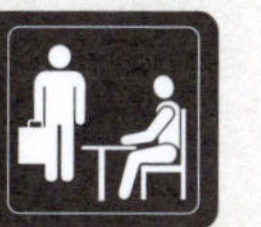

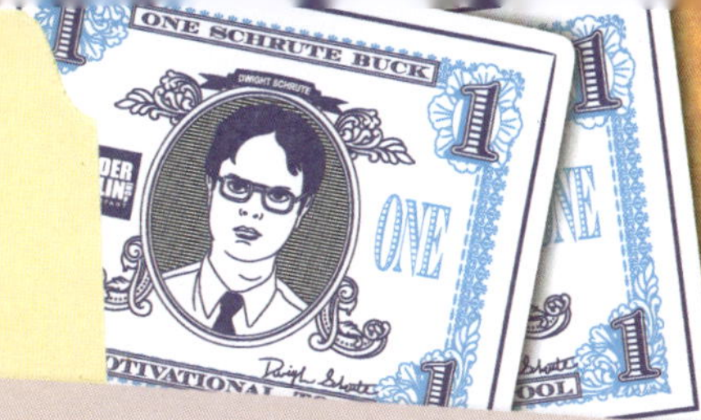

WEEKLY PLAN

NOTES

MONDAY	TUESDAY
WEDNESDAY	THURSDAY
FRIDAY	SATURDAY
	SUNDAY

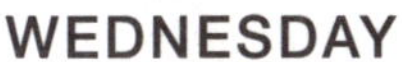

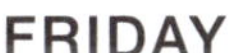

TOP PRIORITIES

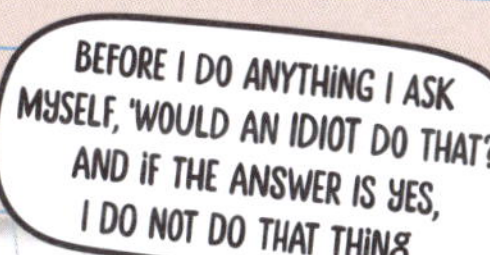

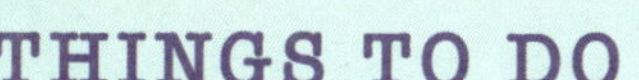

THINGS TO DO

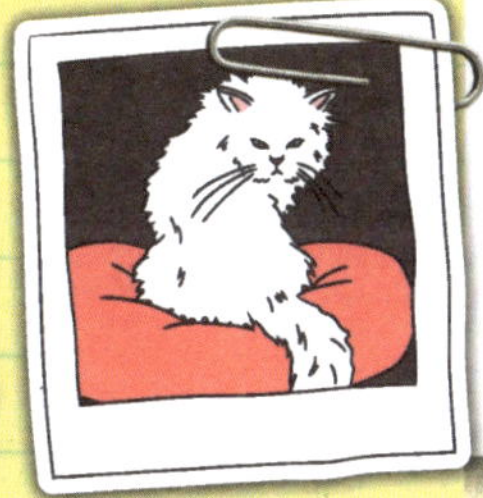

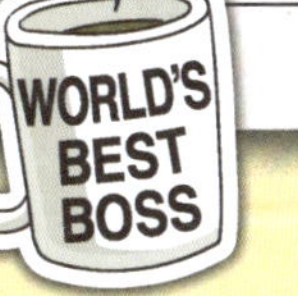

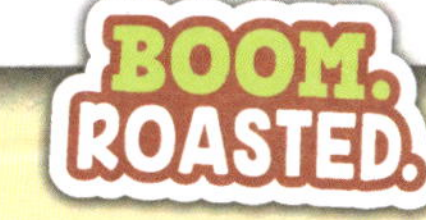

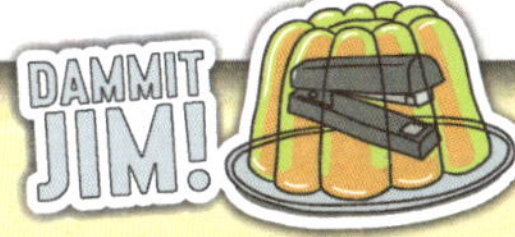

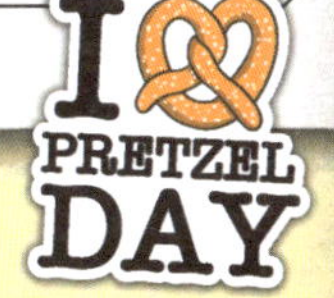

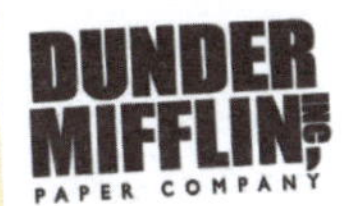

Week of:

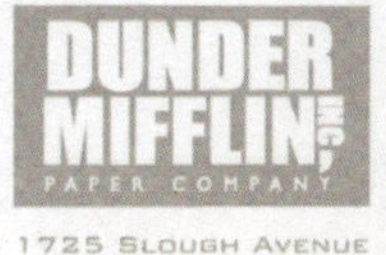

1725 Slough Avenue
Scranton, PA 18505

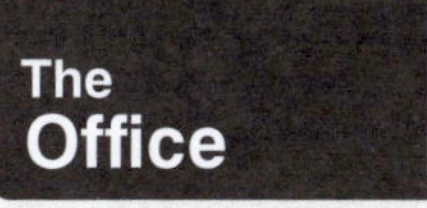

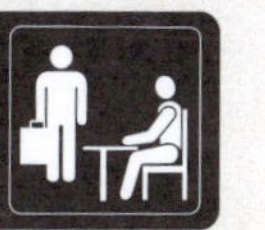

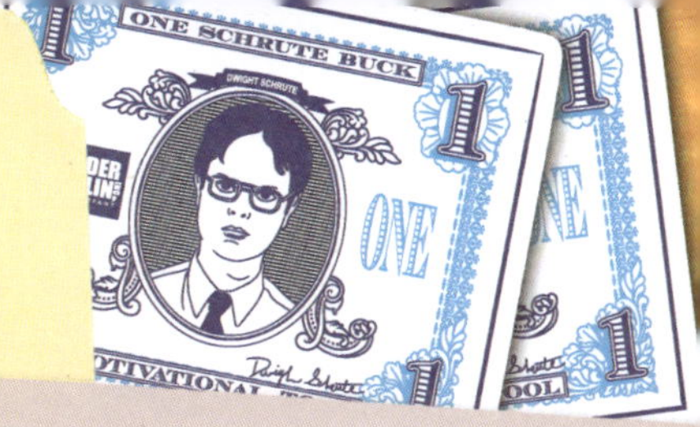

WEEKLY PLAN

NOTES

MONDAY	TUESDAY
WEDNESDAY	**THURSDAY**
FRIDAY	**SATURDAY**
	SUNDAY

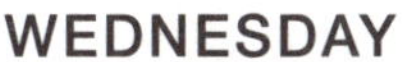

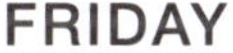

DUNDIE AWARD

TOP PRIORITIES

BEFORE I DO ANYTHING I ASK MYSELF, 'WOULD AN IDIOT DO THAT?' AND IF THE ANSWER IS YES, I DO NOT DO THAT THING.

THINGS TO DO

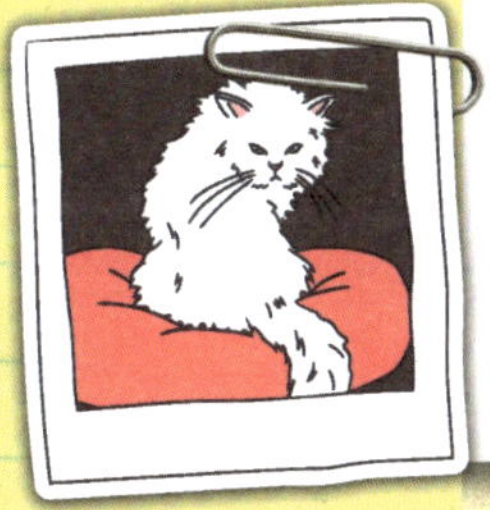

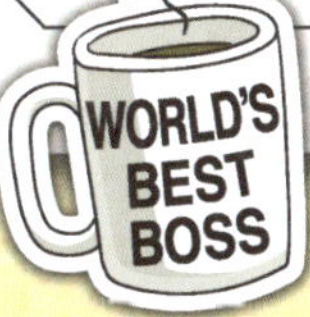

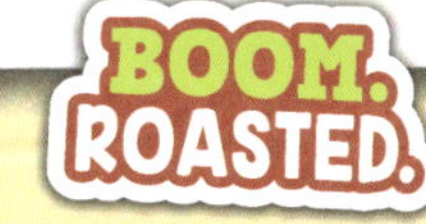

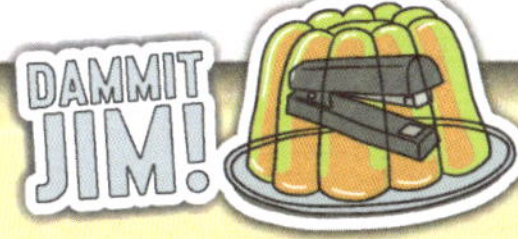

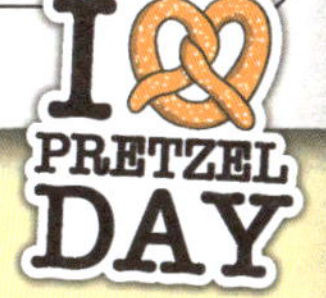

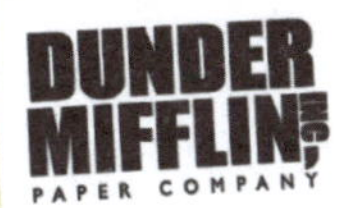

Week of:

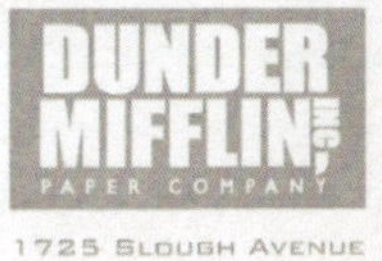

1725 Slough Avenue
Scranton, PA 18505

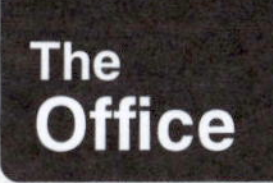

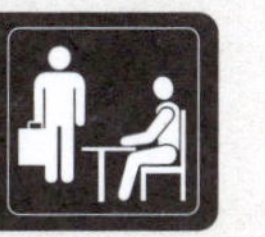

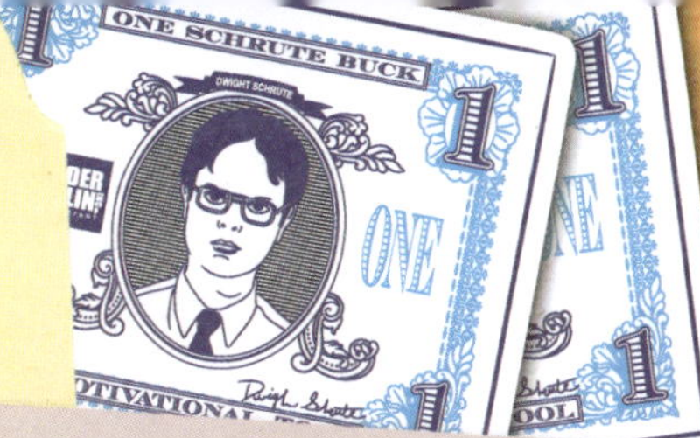

WEEKLY PLAN

NOTES

MONDAY	TUESDAY
WEDNESDAY	THURSDAY
FRIDAY	SATURDAY
	SUNDAY

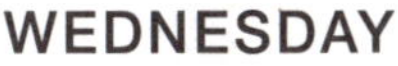

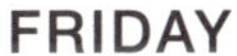

TOP PRIORITIES

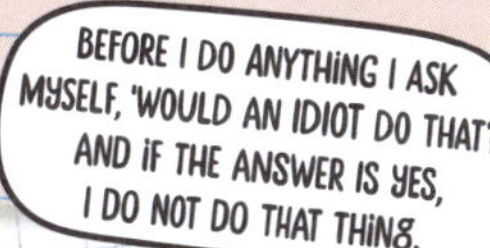

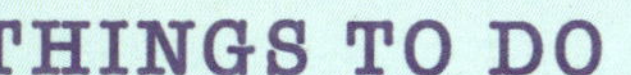

THINGS TO DO

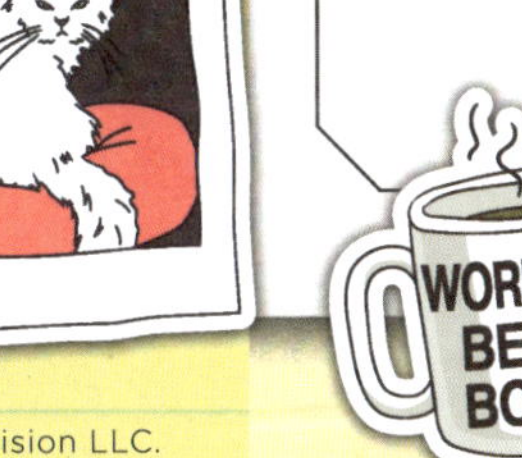

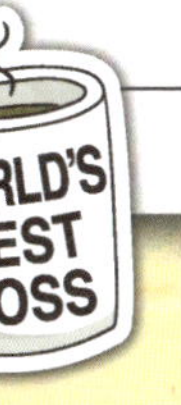

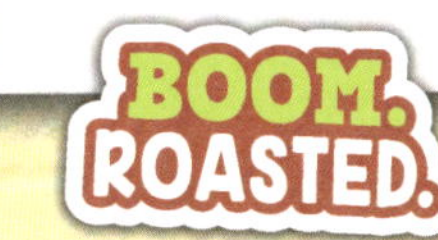

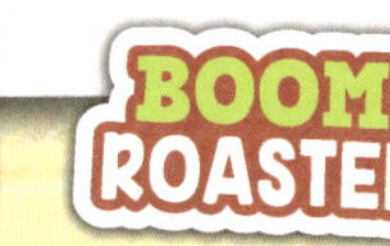

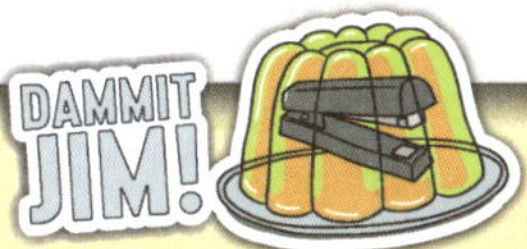

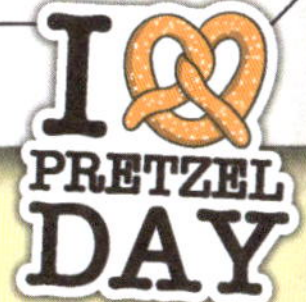

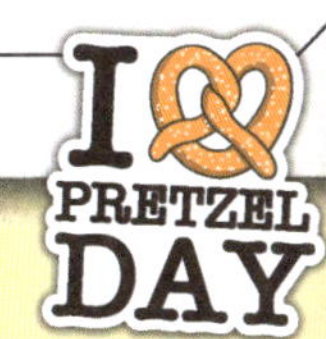

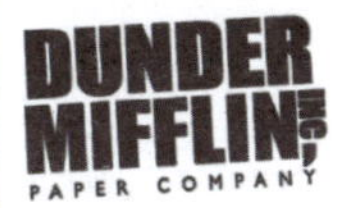

Week of: ______

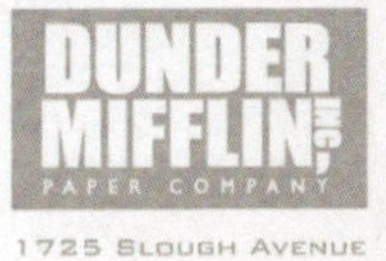

1725 Slough Avenue
Scranton, PA 18505

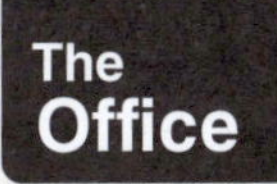

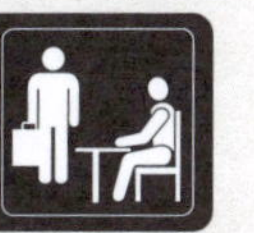

WEEKLY PLAN

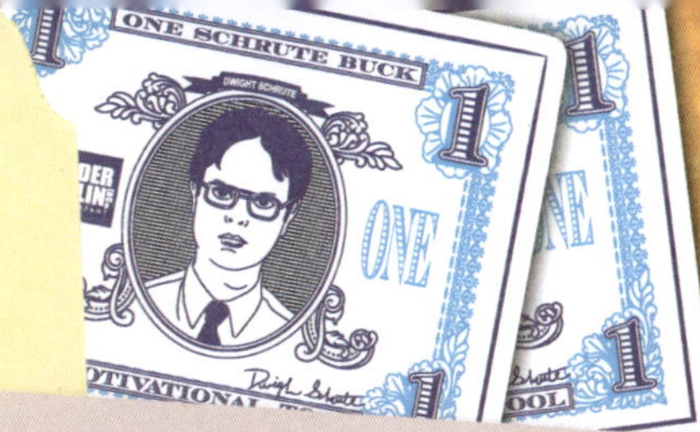

NOTES

MONDAY	TUESDAY
WEDNESDAY	THURSDAY
FRIDAY	SATURDAY
	SUNDAY

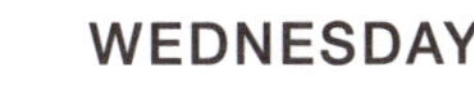

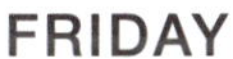

TOP PRIORITIES

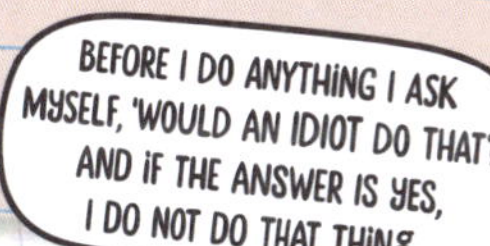

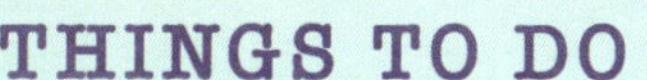

THINGS TO DO

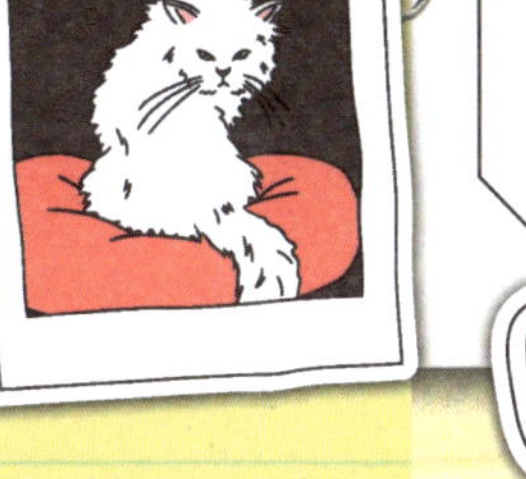

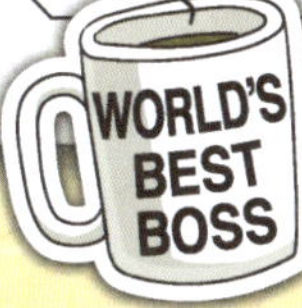

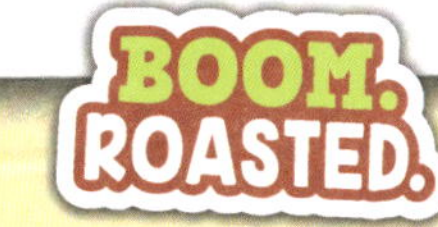

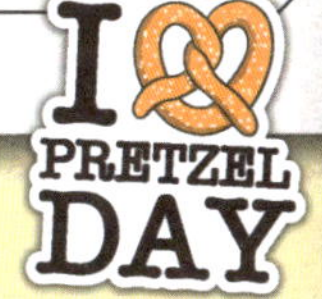

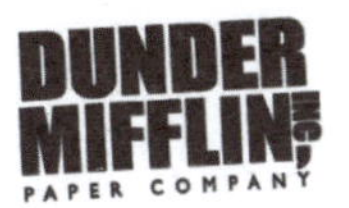

Week of:

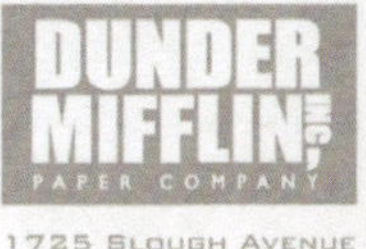

1725 Slough Avenue
Scranton, PA 18505

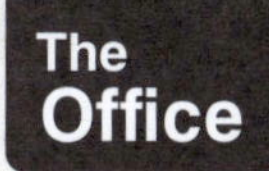

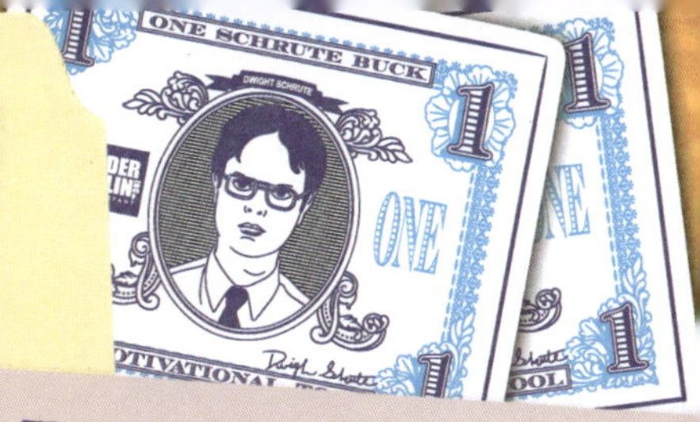

WEEKLY PLAN

NOTES

MONDAY	TUESDAY
WEDNESDAY	THURSDAY
FRIDAY	SATURDAY
	SUNDAY

TOP PRIORITIES

BEFORE I DO ANYTHING I ASK MYSELF, 'WOULD AN IDIOT DO THAT?' AND IF THE ANSWER IS YES, I DO NOT DO THAT THING.

THINGS TO DO

DUNDIE AWARD

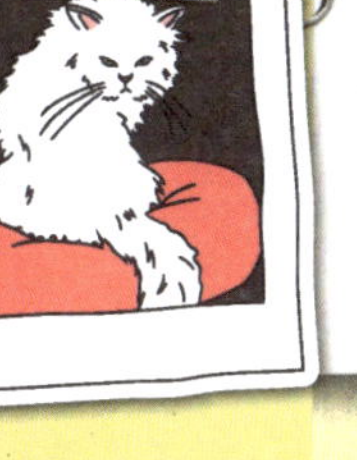

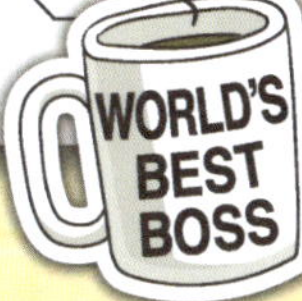

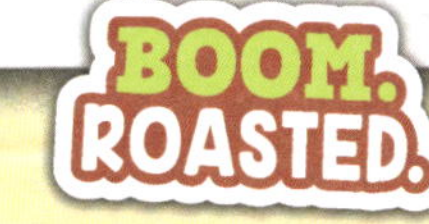

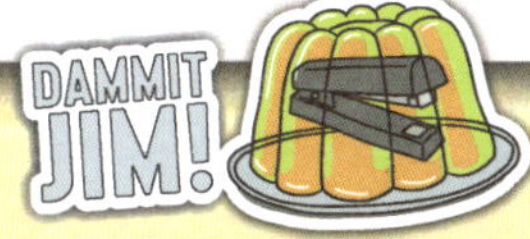

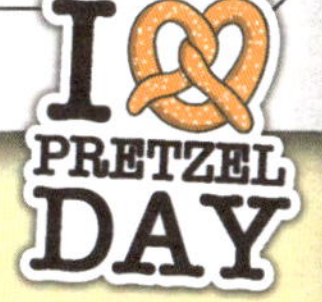

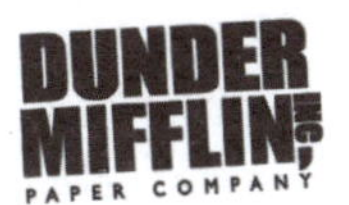

Week of:

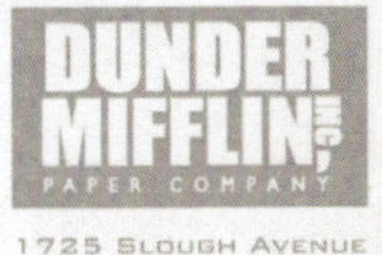

1725 Slough Avenue
Scranton, PA 18505

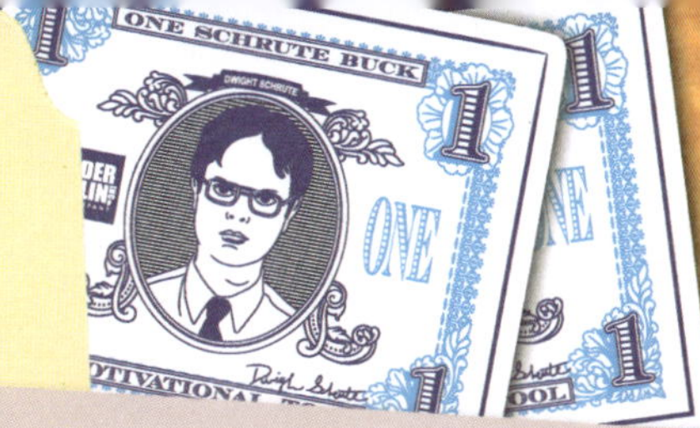

WEEKLY PLAN

NOTES

MONDAY	TUESDAY
WEDNESDAY	THURSDAY
FRIDAY	SATURDAY
	SUNDAY

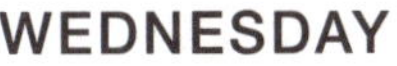
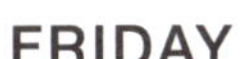

TOP PRIORITIES

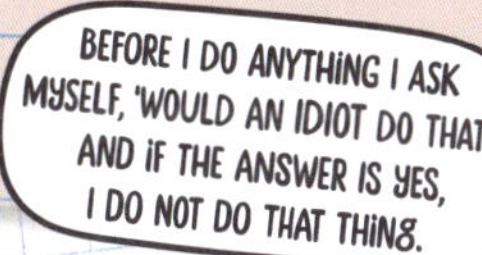
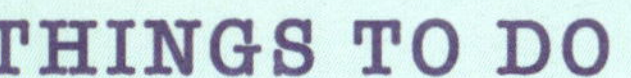

BEFORE I DO ANYTHING I ASK MYSELF, 'WOULD AN IDIOT DO THAT?' AND IF THE ANSWER IS YES, I DO NOT DO THAT THING.

THINGS TO DO

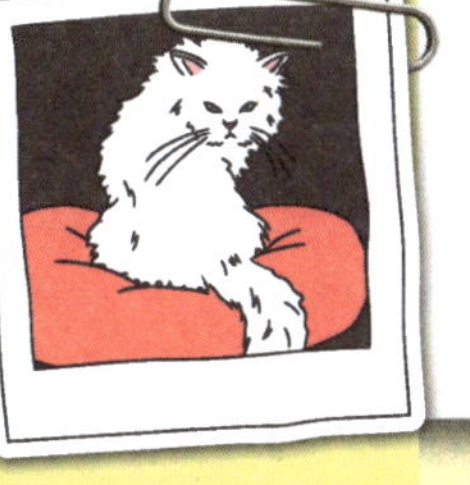
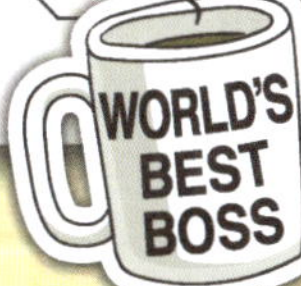

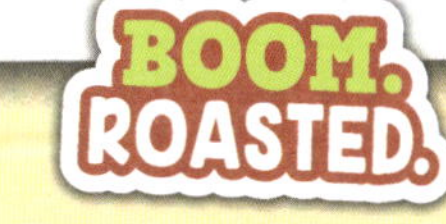

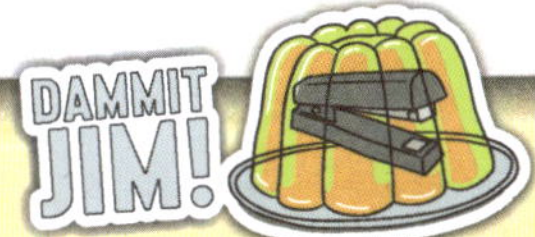

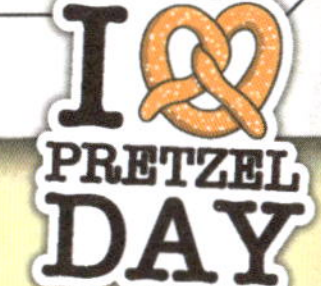

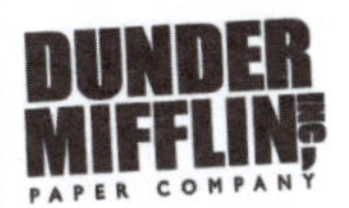

Week of:

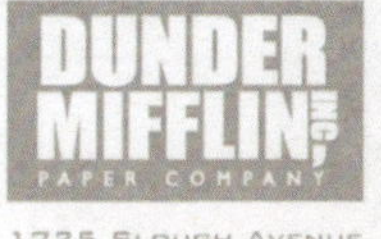

1725 Slough Avenue
Scranton, PA 18505

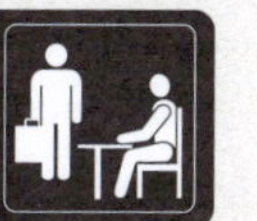

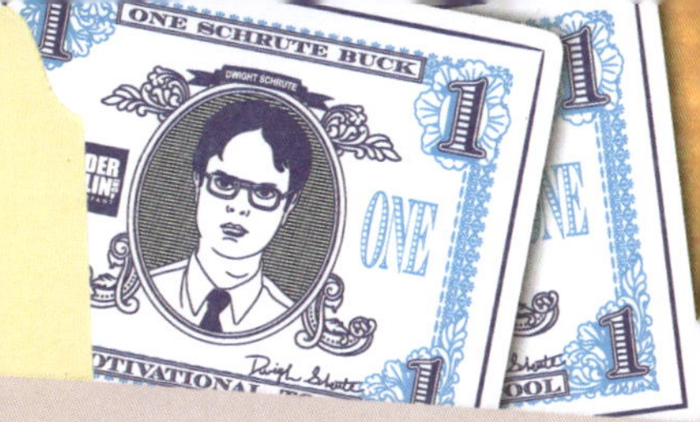

WEEKLY PLAN

NOTES

MONDAY	TUESDAY
WEDNESDAY	**THURSDAY**
FRIDAY	**SATURDAY**
	SUNDAY

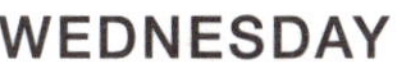

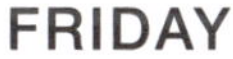

TOP PRIORITIES

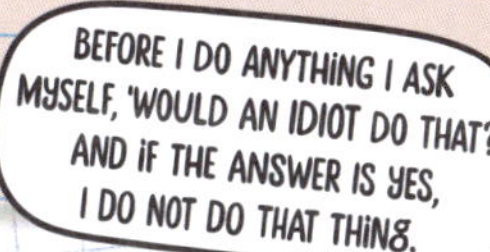

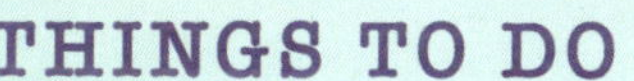

THINGS TO DO

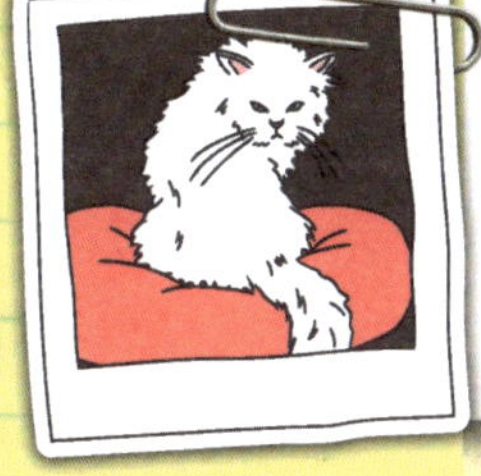

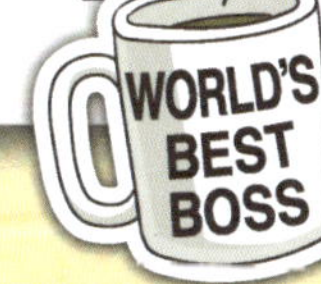

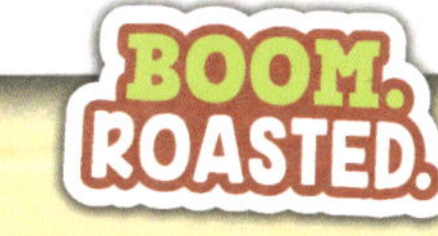

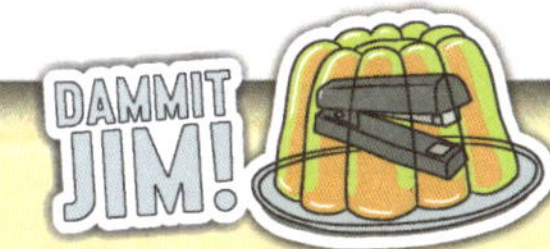

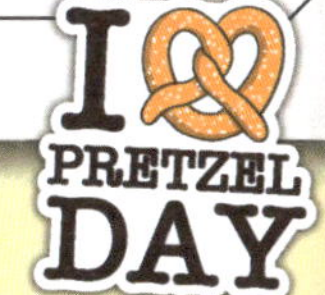

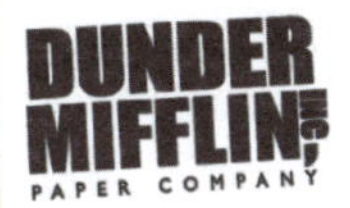

Week of:

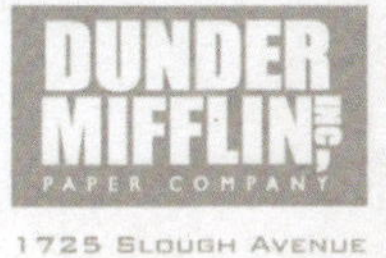

1725 Slough Avenue
Scranton, PA 18505

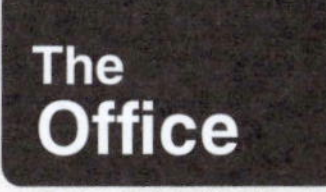

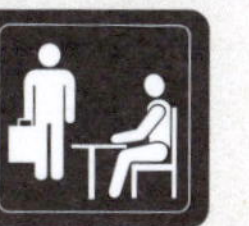

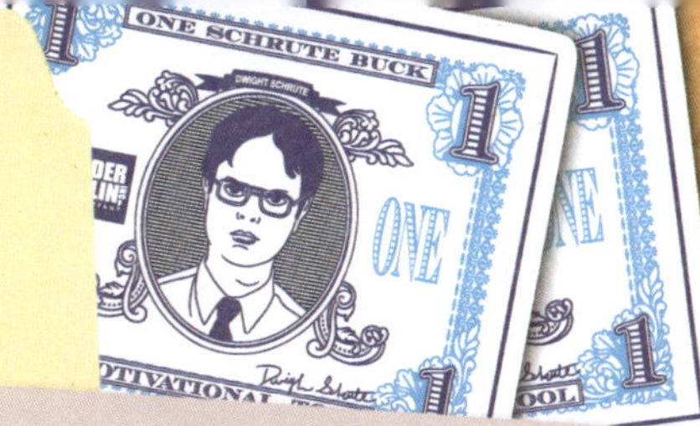

WEEKLY PLAN

NOTES

MONDAY	TUESDAY
WEDNESDAY	**THURSDAY**
FRIDAY	**SATURDAY**
	SUNDAY

DUNDIE AWARD

TOP PRIORITIES

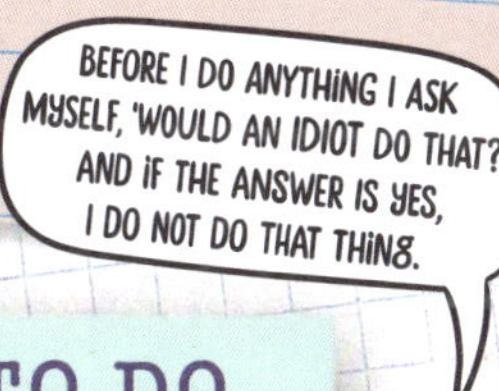

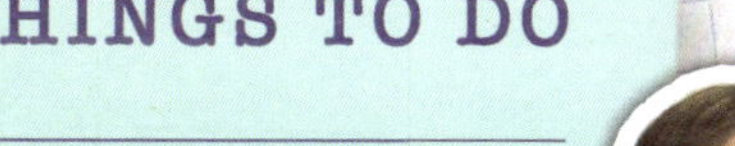

THINGS TO DO

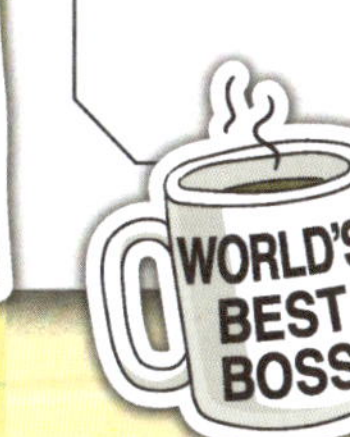

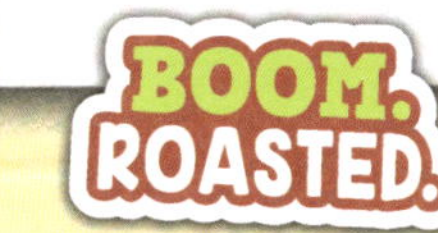

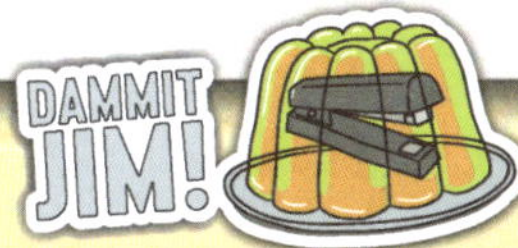

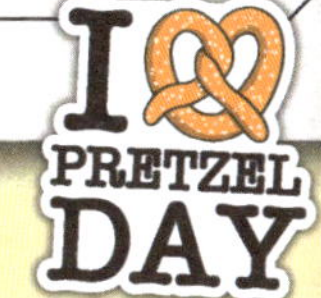

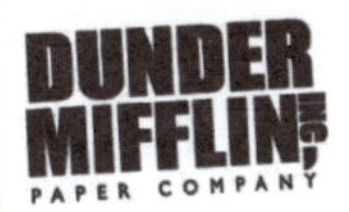

Week of:

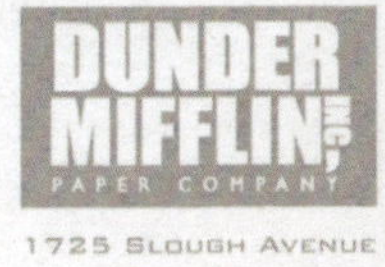

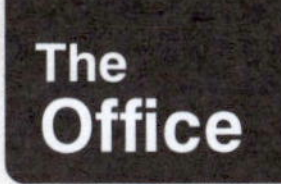

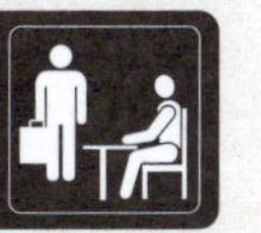

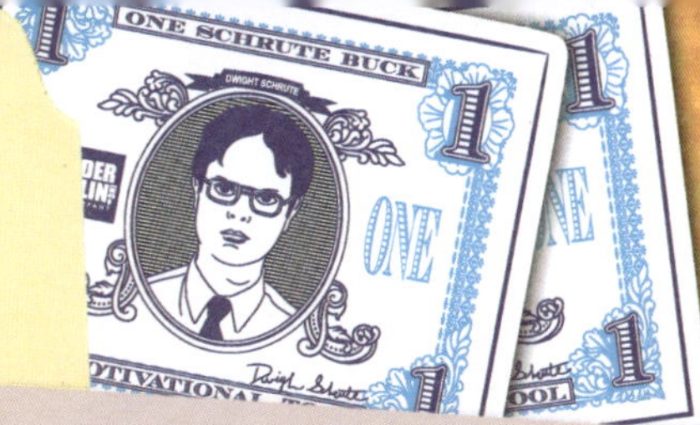

WEEKLY PLAN

NOTES

MONDAY	TUESDAY
WEDNESDAY	THURSDAY
FRIDAY	SATURDAY
	SUNDAY

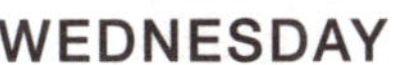

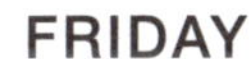

TOP PRIORITIES

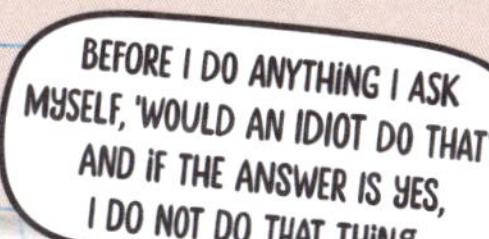

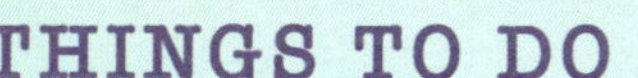

THINGS TO DO

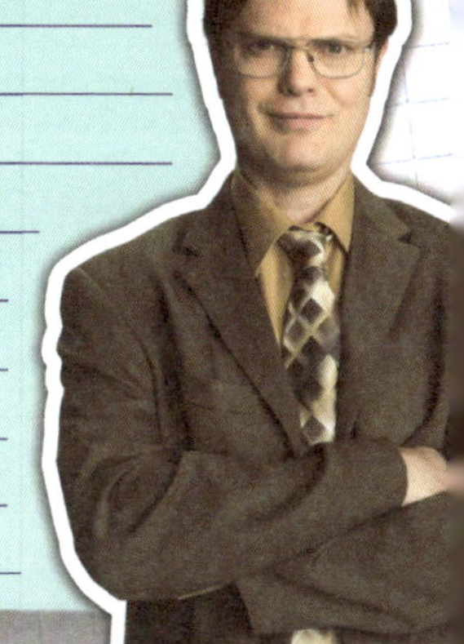

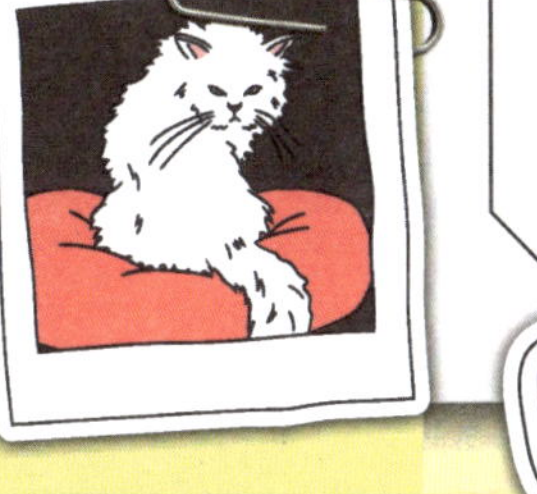

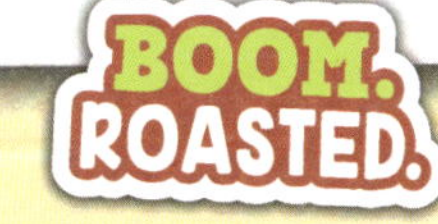

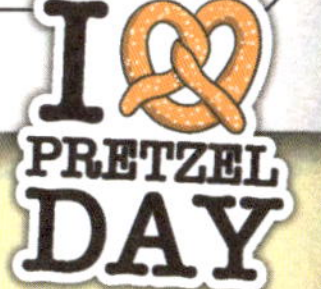

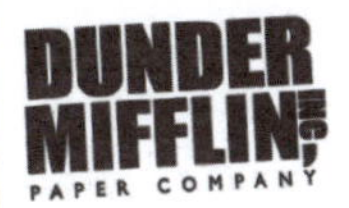

Week of:

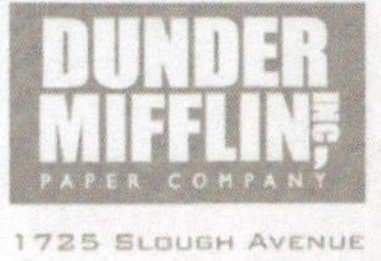

1725 Slough Avenue
Scranton, PA 18505

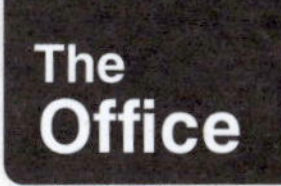

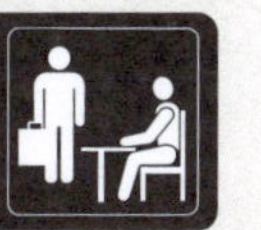

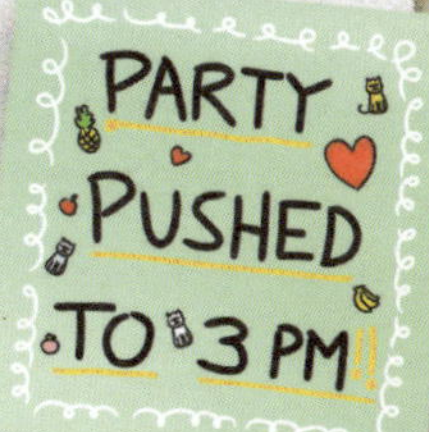

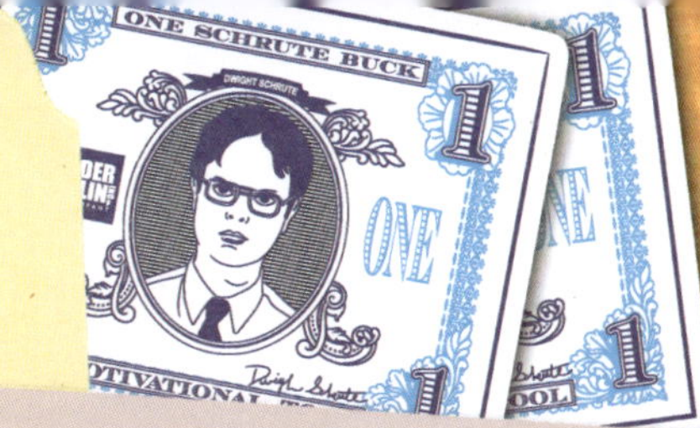

WEEKLY PLAN

NOTES

MONDAY	TUESDAY

WEDNESDAY	THURSDAY

FRIDAY	SATURDAY
	SUNDAY

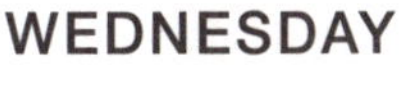

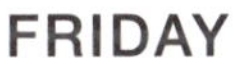

TOP PRIORITIES

BEFORE I DO ANYTHING I ASK MYSELF, 'WOULD AN IDIOT DO THAT?' AND IF THE ANSWER IS YES, I DO NOT DO THAT THING.

THINGS TO DO

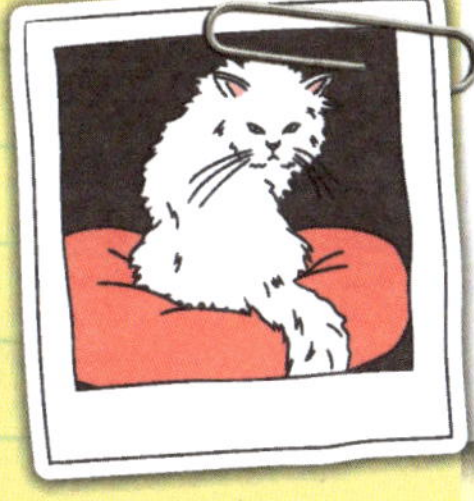

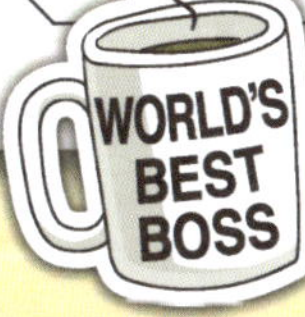

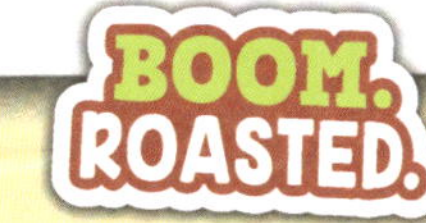

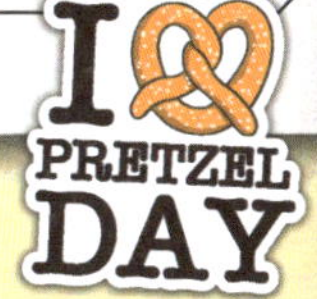

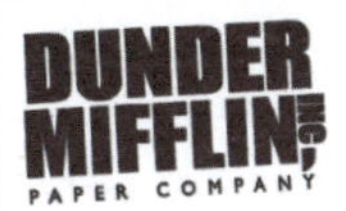

Week of:

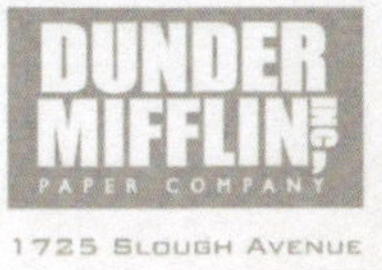

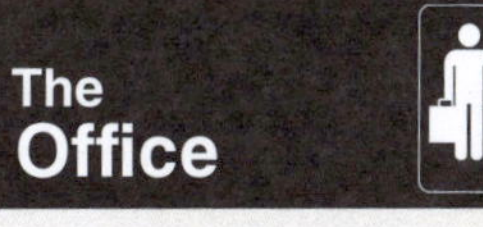

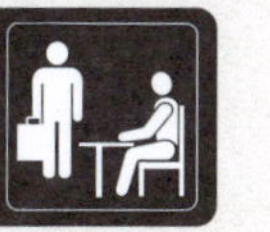

1725 Slough Avenue
Scranton, PA 18505

WEEKLY PLAN

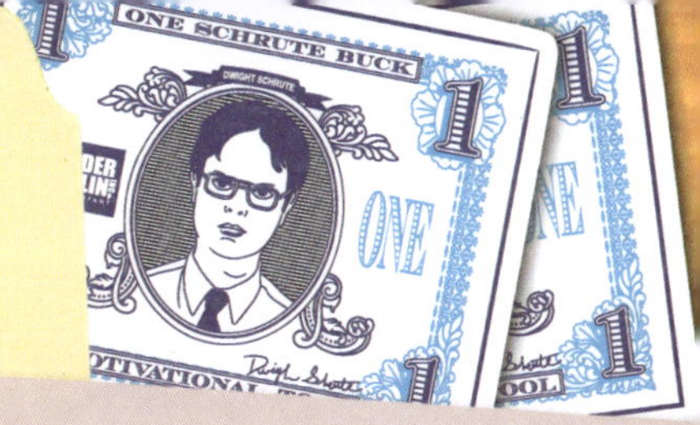

NOTES

TOP PRIORITIES

MONDAY	TUESDAY
WEDNESDAY	THURSDAY
FRIDAY	SATURDAY
	SUNDAY

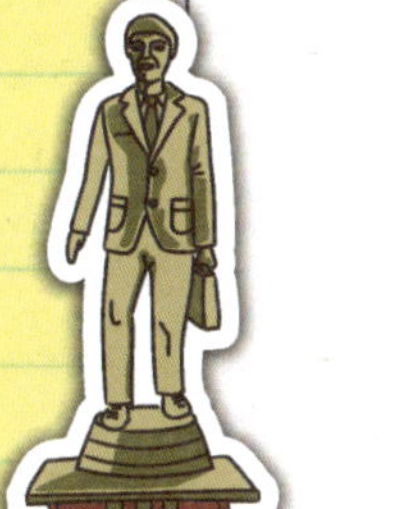

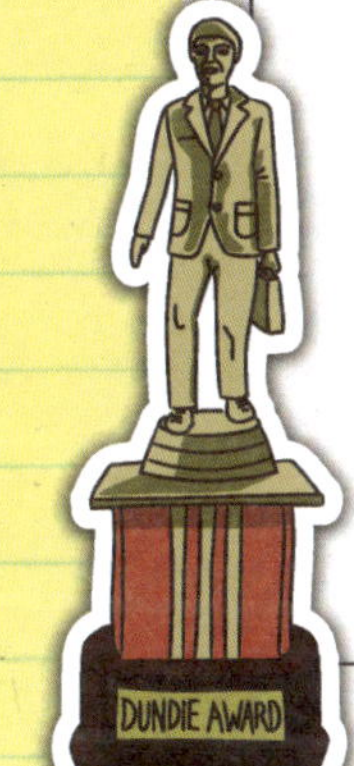

BEFORE I DO ANYTHING I ASK MYSELF, 'WOULD AN IDIOT DO THAT?' AND IF THE ANSWER IS YES, I DO NOT DO THAT THING.

THINGS TO DO

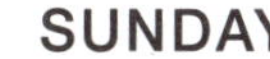

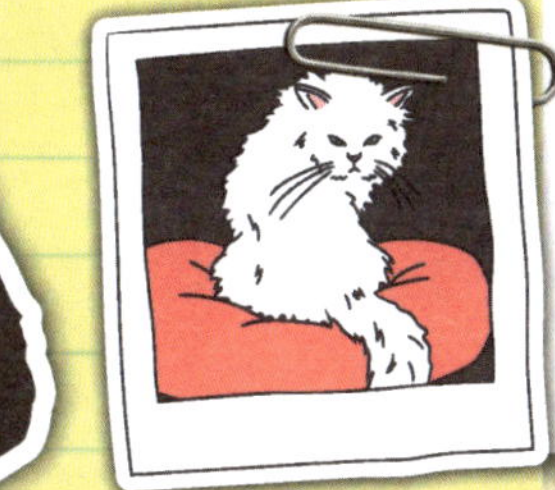

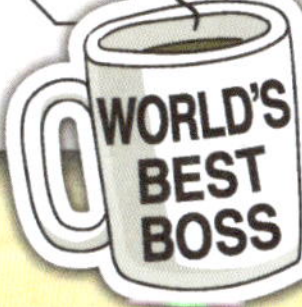

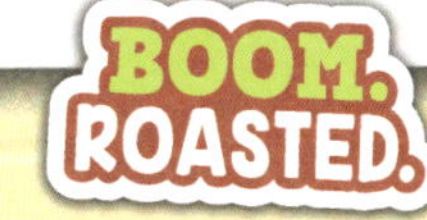

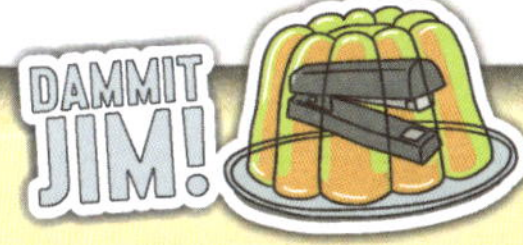

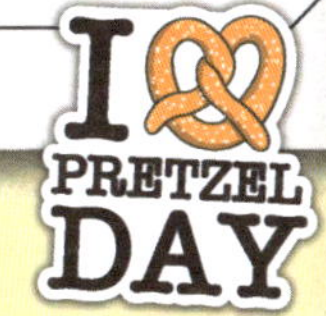

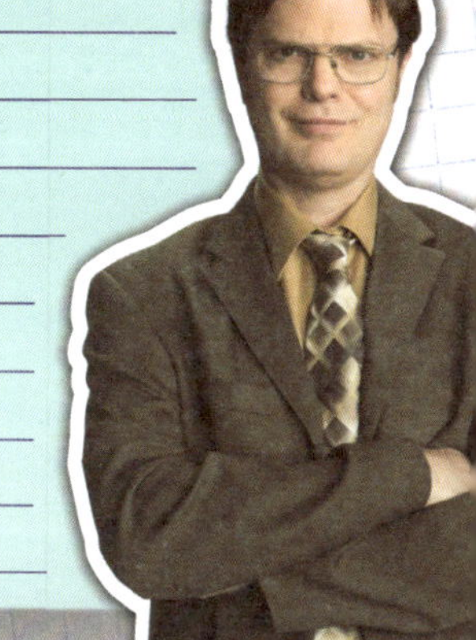

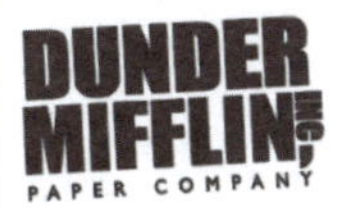

Week of:

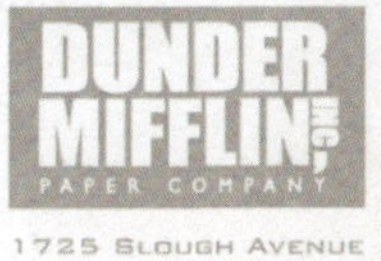

1725 Slough Avenue
Scranton, PA 18505

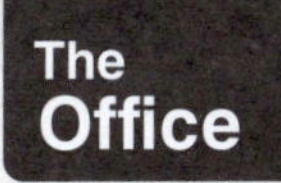

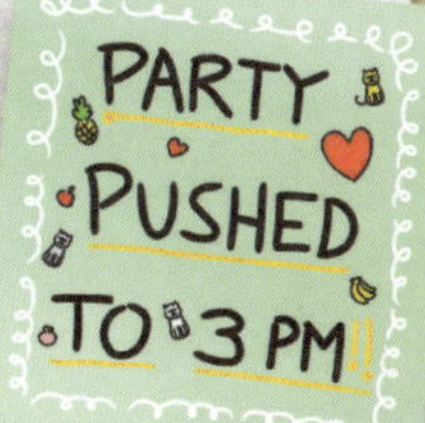

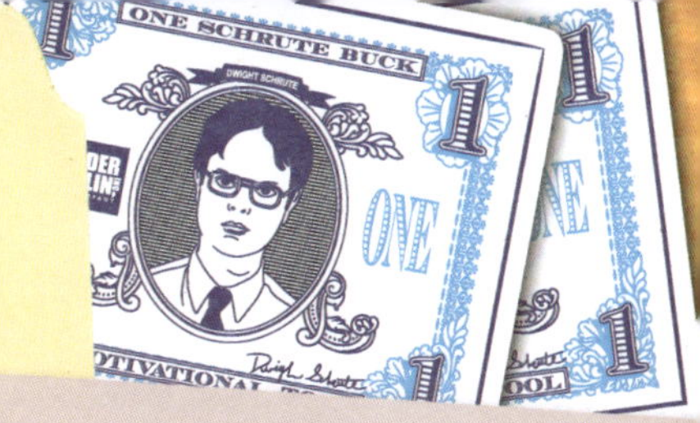

WEEKLY PLAN

NOTES

MONDAY	TUESDAY
WEDNESDAY	THURSDAY
FRIDAY	SATURDAY
	SUNDAY

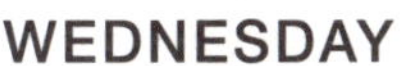

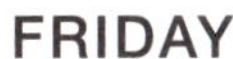

TOP PRIORITIES

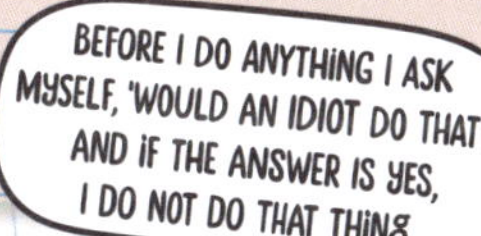

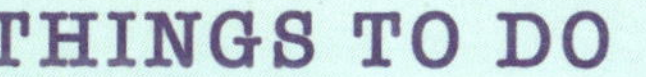

THINGS TO DO

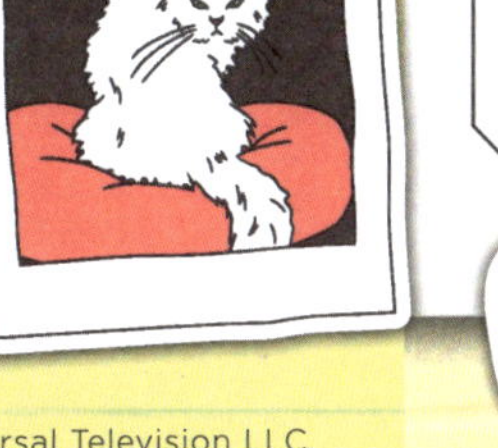

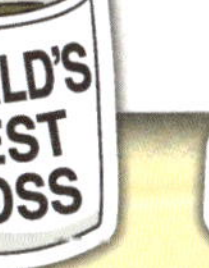

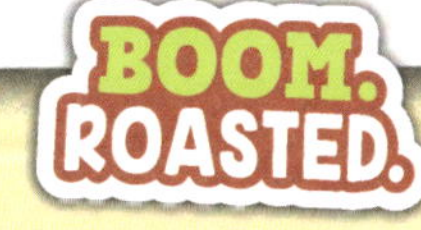

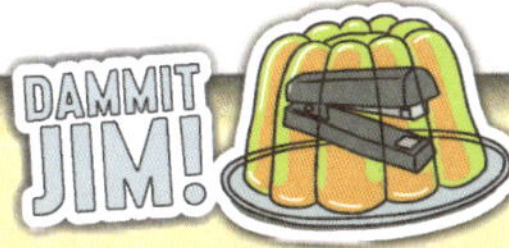

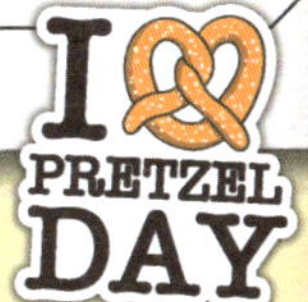

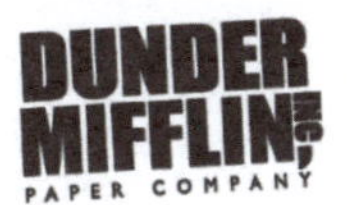

Week of: ____________

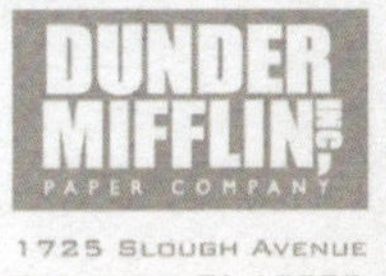

1725 Slough Avenue
Scranton, PA 18505

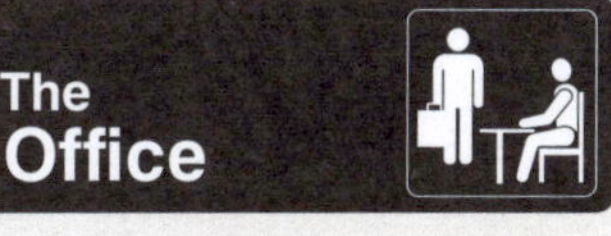

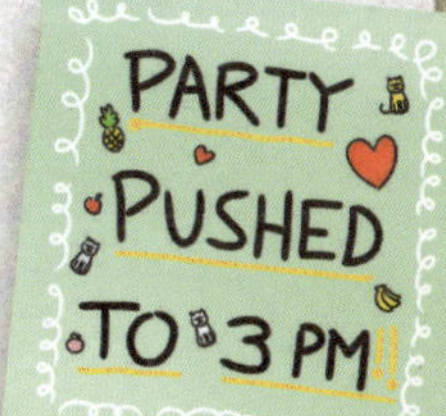

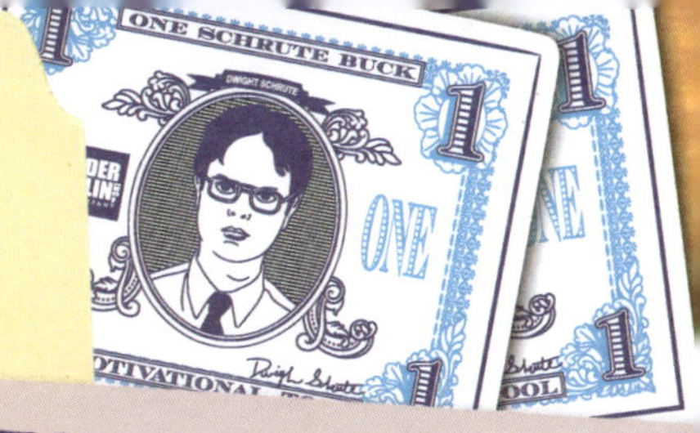

WEEKLY PLAN

NOTES

MONDAY	TUESDAY
WEDNESDAY	THURSDAY
FRIDAY	SATURDAY
	SUNDAY

TOP PRIORITIES

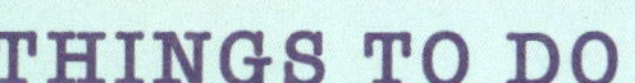

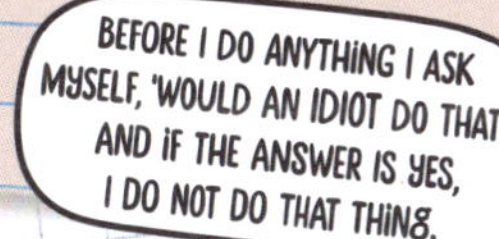

THINGS TO DO

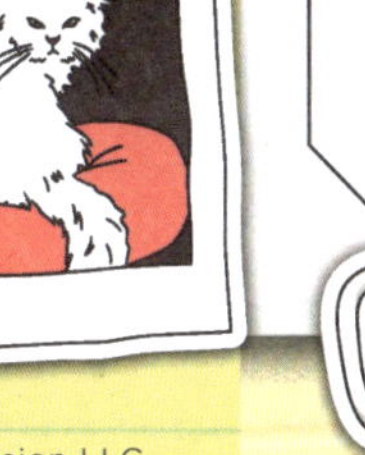

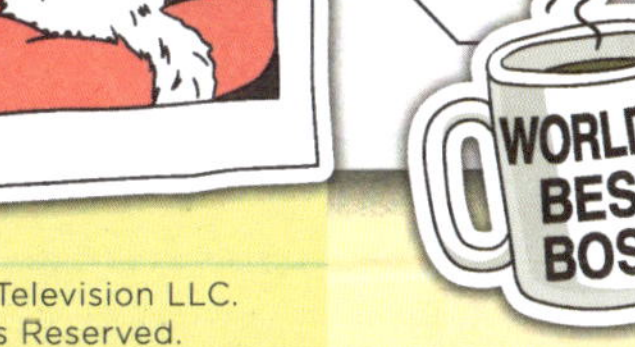

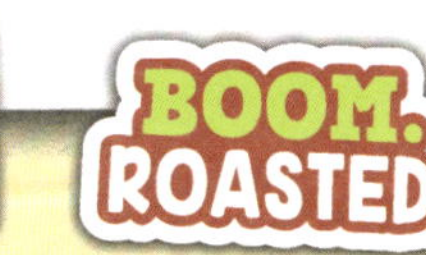

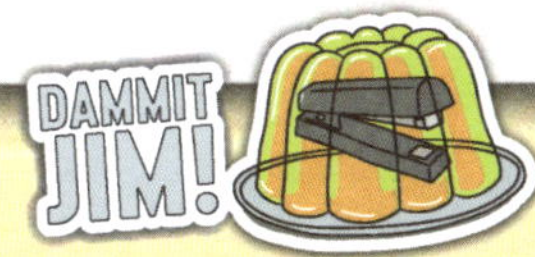

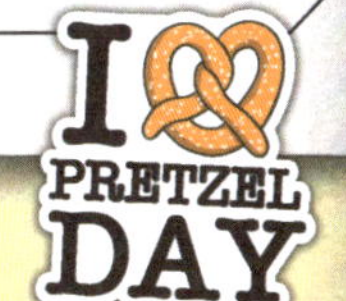

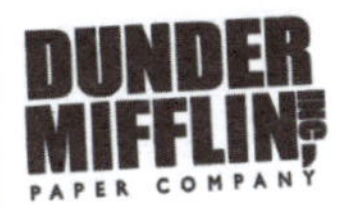

Week of:

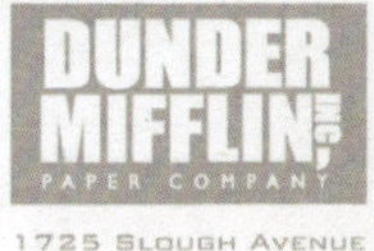

1725 Slough Avenue
Scranton, PA 18505

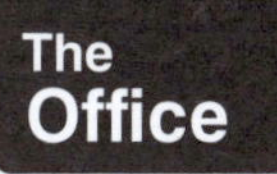

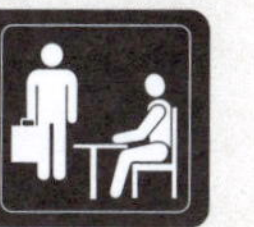

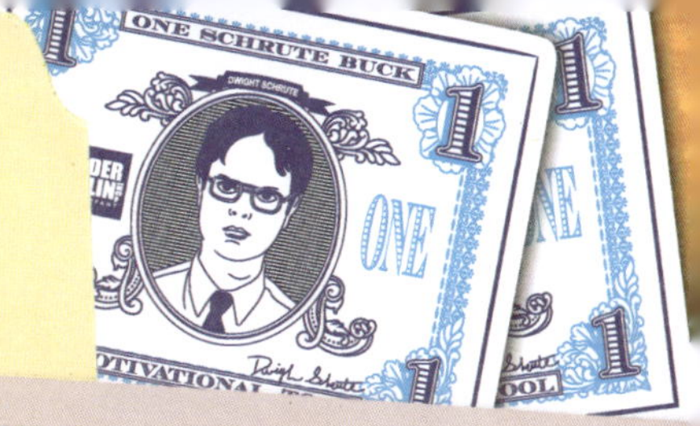

WEEKLY PLAN

NOTES

MONDAY	TUESDAY
WEDNESDAY	THURSDAY
FRIDAY	SATURDAY
	SUNDAY

DUNDIE AWARD

TOP PRIORITIES

BEFORE I DO ANYTHING I ASK MYSELF, 'WOULD AN IDIOT DO THAT?' AND IF THE ANSWER IS YES, I DO NOT DO THAT THING.

THINGS TO DO

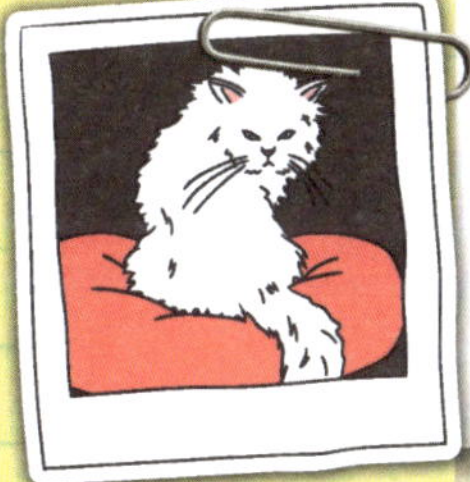

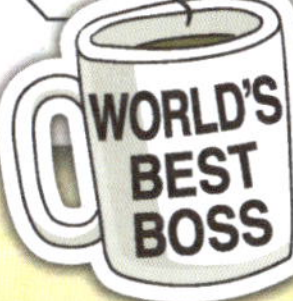

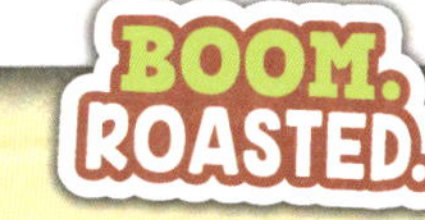

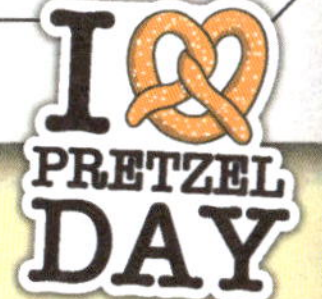

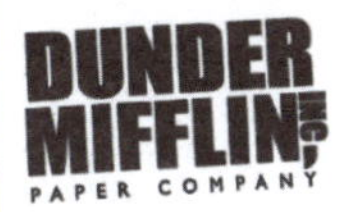

Week of:

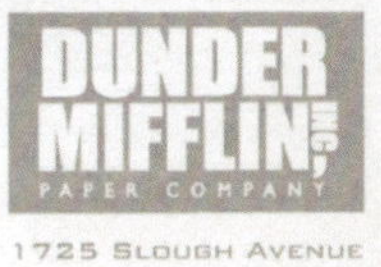

1725 Slough Avenue
Scranton, PA 18505

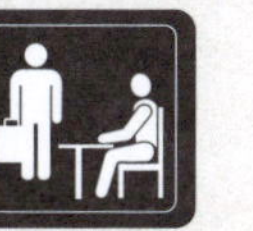

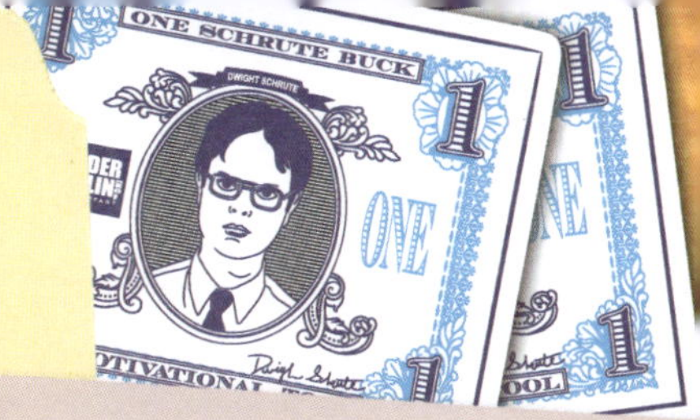

WEEKLY PLAN

NOTES

MONDAY	TUESDAY
WEDNESDAY	THURSDAY
FRIDAY	SATURDAY
	SUNDAY

TOP PRIORITIES

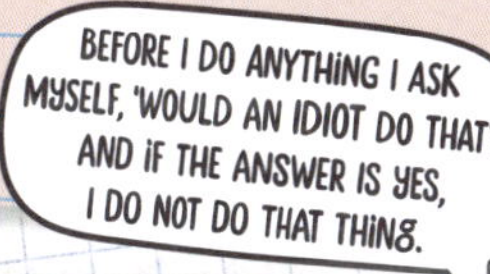

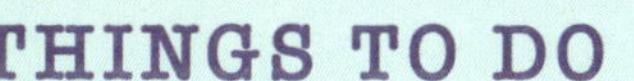

DUNDIE AWARD

THINGS TO DO

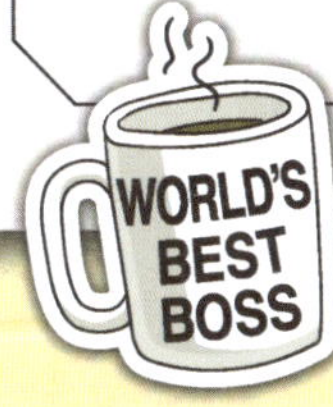
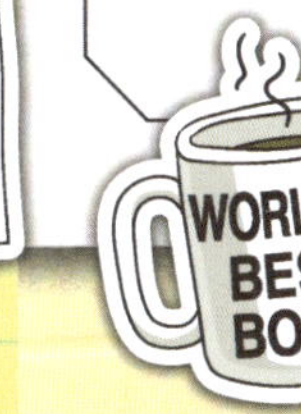

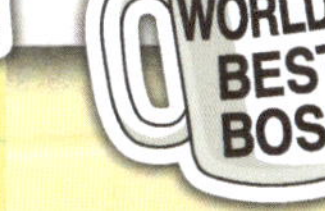
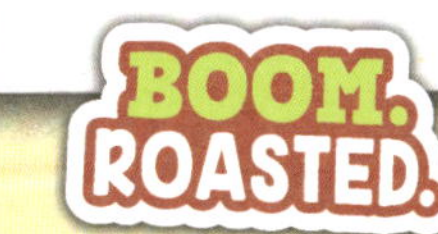

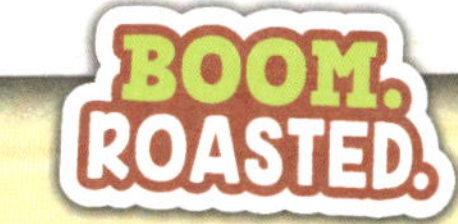
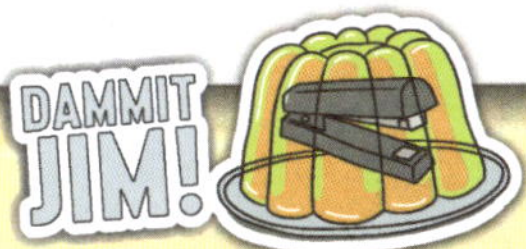

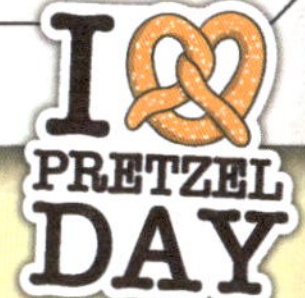

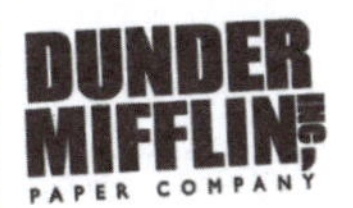

Week of:

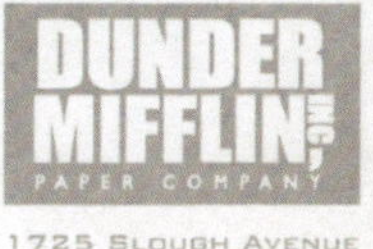

1725 Slough Avenue
Scranton, PA 18505

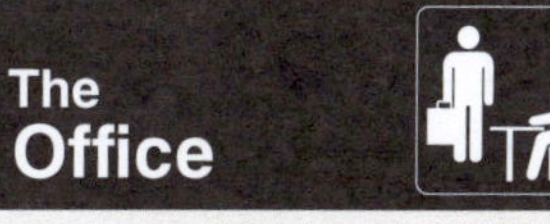

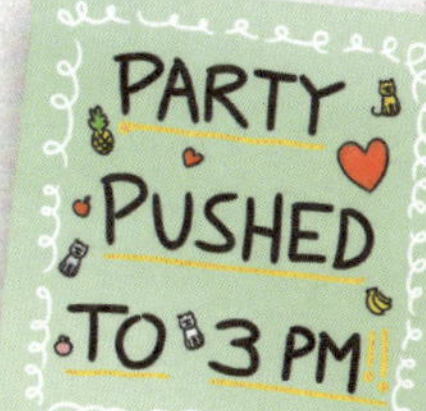

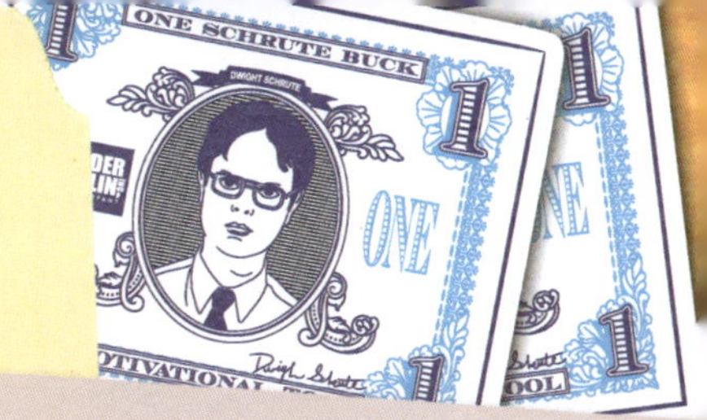

WEEKLY PLAN

NOTES

MONDAY	TUESDAY
WEDNESDAY	THURSDAY
FRIDAY	SATURDAY
	SUNDAY

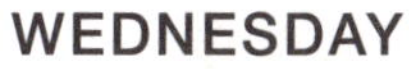
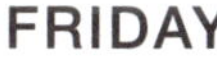

TOP PRIORITIES

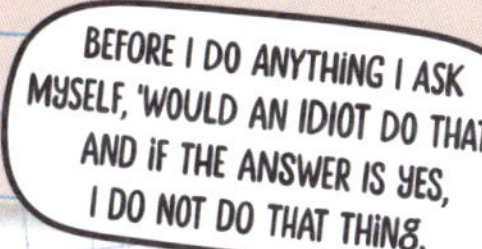

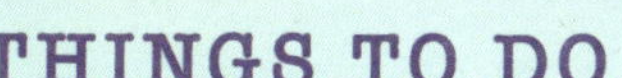

THINGS TO DO

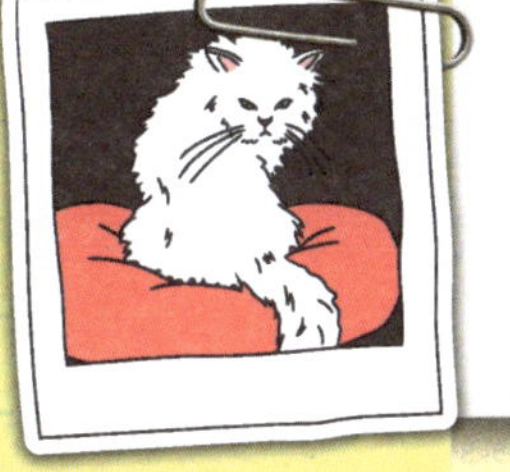

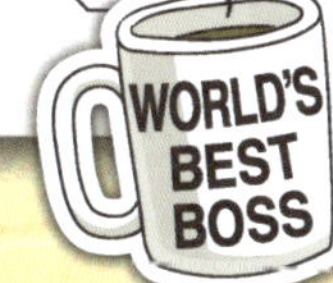

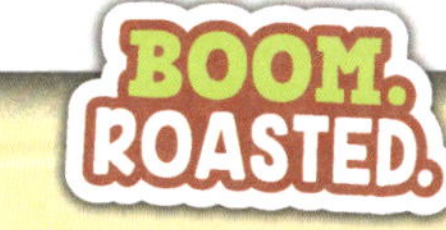

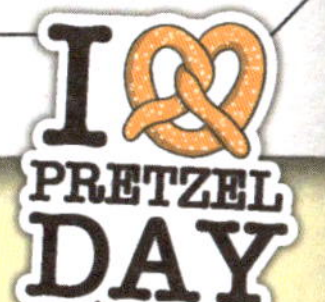

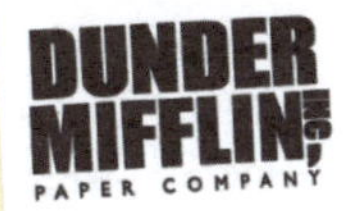

Week of:

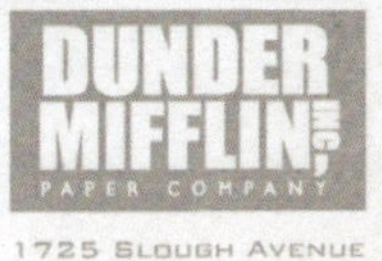

1725 Slough Avenue
Scranton, PA 18505

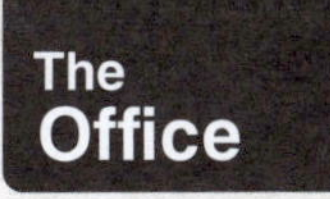

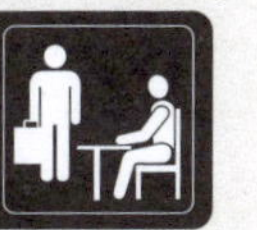

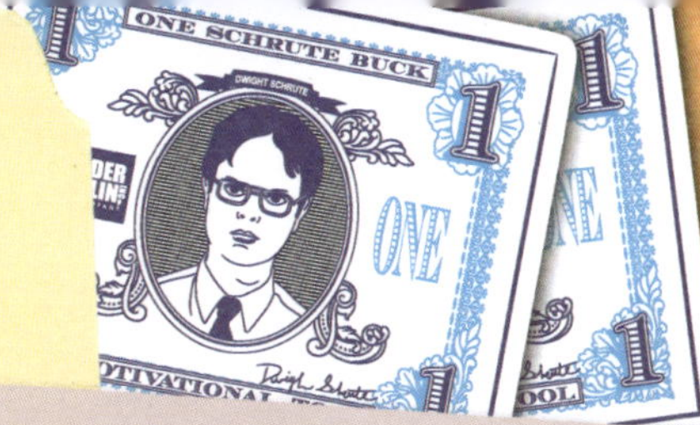

WEEKLY PLAN

NOTES

MONDAY	TUESDAY
WEDNESDAY	THURSDAY
FRIDAY	SATURDAY
	SUNDAY

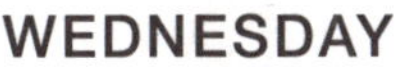

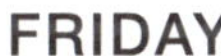

DUNDIE AWARD

TOP PRIORITIES

BEFORE I DO ANYTHING I ASK MYSELF, 'WOULD AN IDIOT DO THAT?' AND IF THE ANSWER IS YES, I DO NOT DO THAT THING.

THINGS TO DO

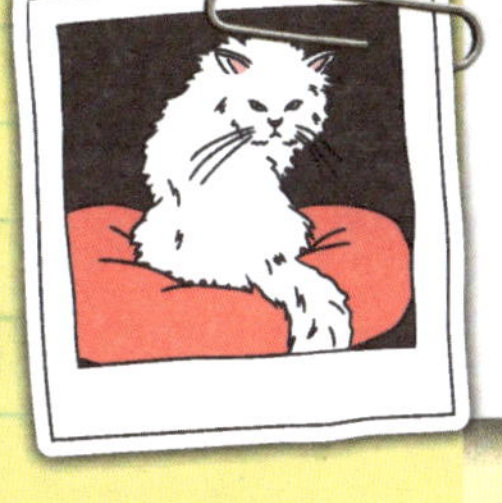

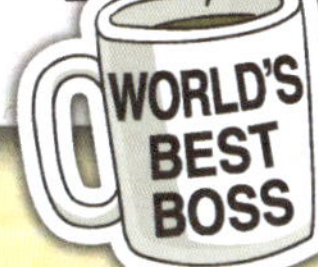

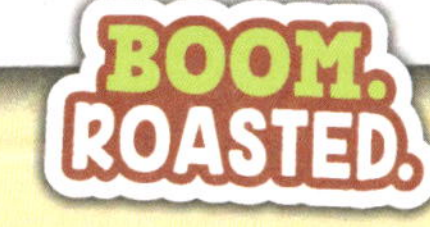

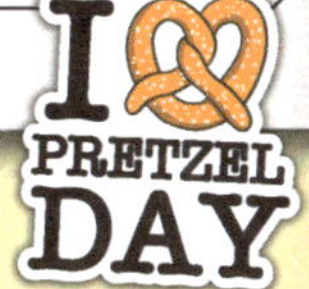

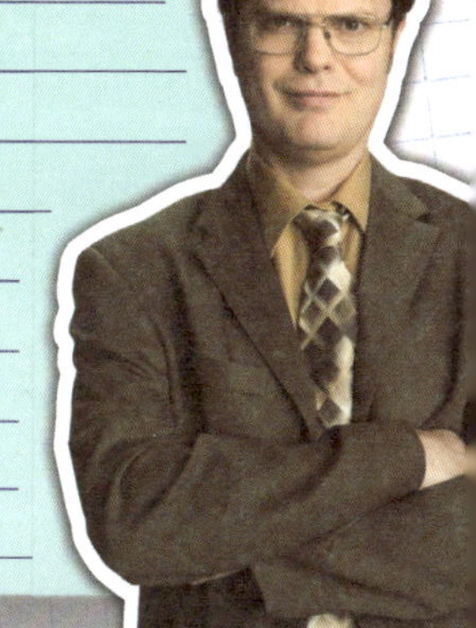

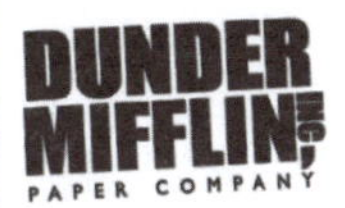

Week of:

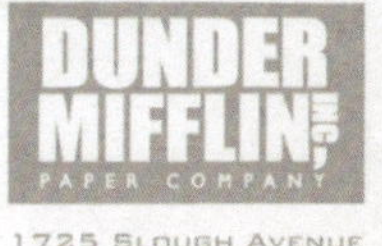

1725 Slough Avenue
Scranton, PA 18505

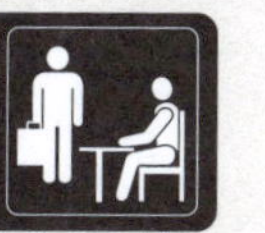

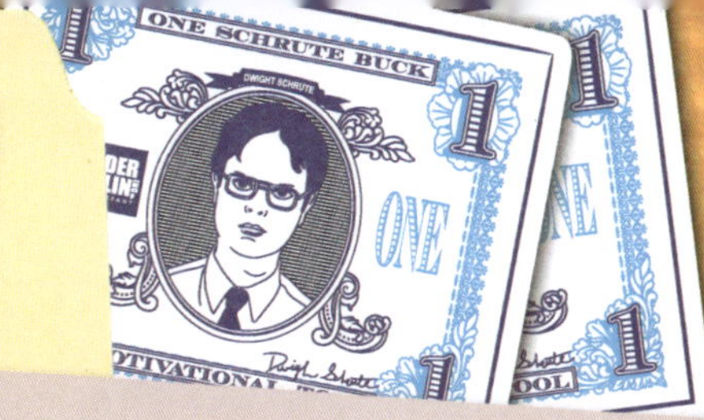

WEEKLY PLAN

NOTES

MONDAY	TUESDAY
WEDNESDAY	THURSDAY
FRIDAY	SATURDAY
	SUNDAY

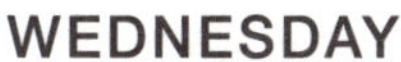
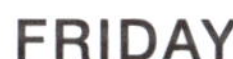

TOP PRIORITIES

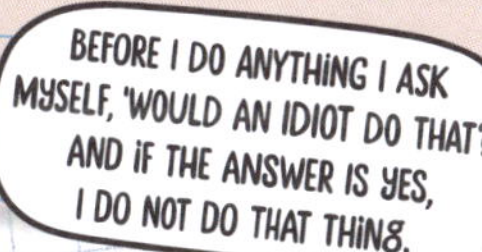
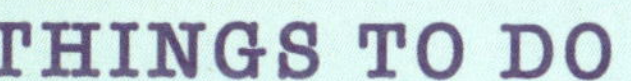

BEFORE I DO ANYTHING I ASK MYSELF, 'WOULD AN IDIOT DO THAT?' AND IF THE ANSWER IS YES, I DO NOT DO THAT THING.

THINGS TO DO

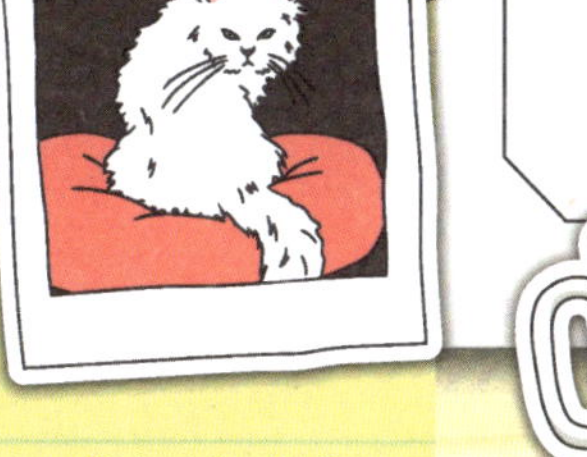
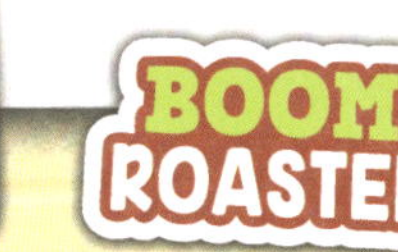

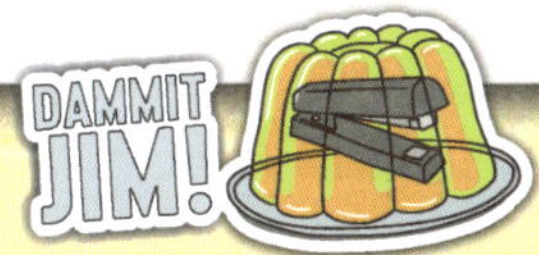

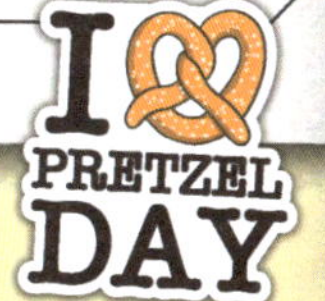

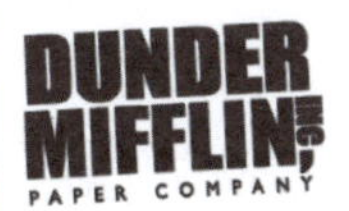

Week of:

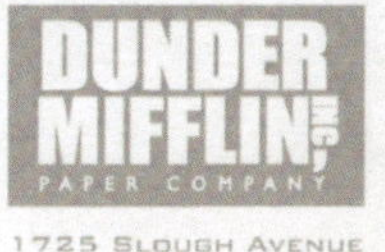

1725 Slough Avenue
Scranton, PA 18505

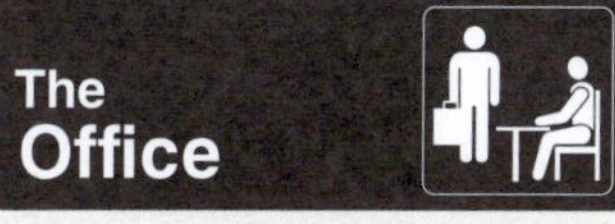

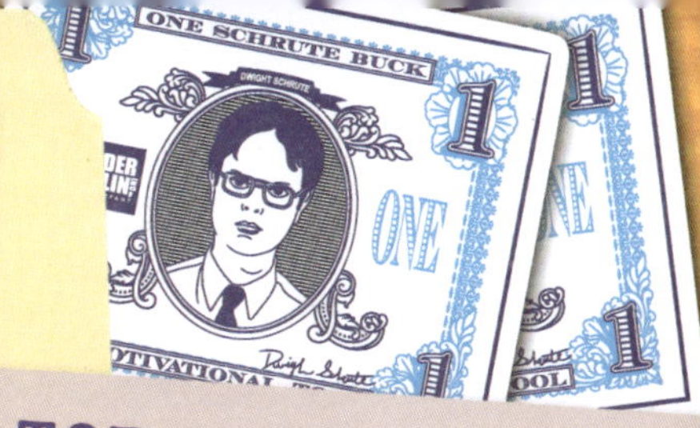

WEEKLY PLAN

NOTES

MONDAY	TUESDAY
WEDNESDAY	THURSDAY
FRIDAY	SATURDAY SUNDAY

DUNDIE AWARD

TOP PRIORITIES

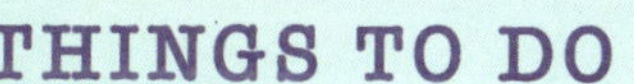

BEFORE I DO ANYTHING I ASK MYSELF, 'WOULD AN IDIOT DO THAT?' AND IF THE ANSWER IS YES, I DO NOT DO THAT THING.

THINGS TO DO

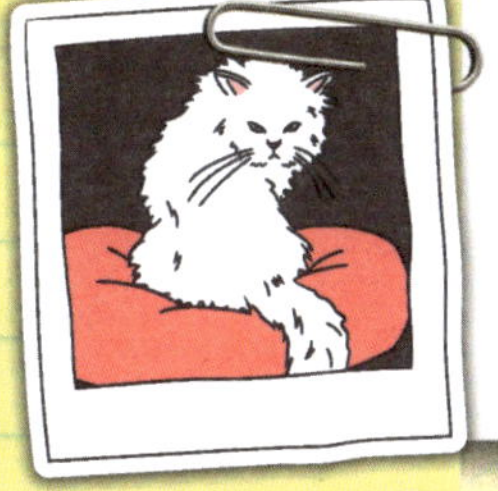

WORLD'S BEST BOSS

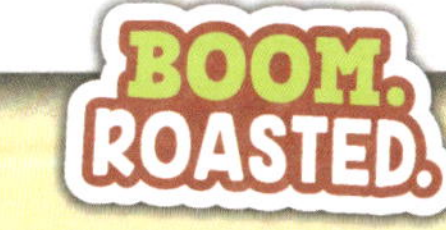

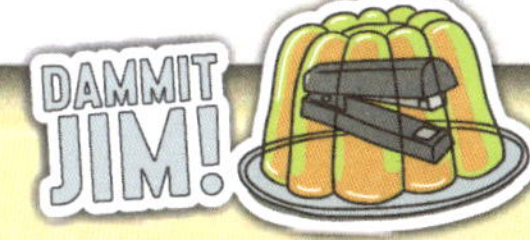

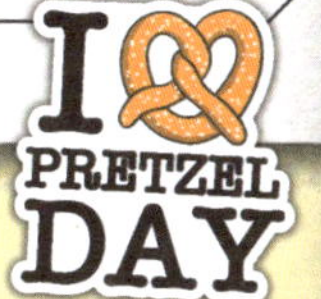

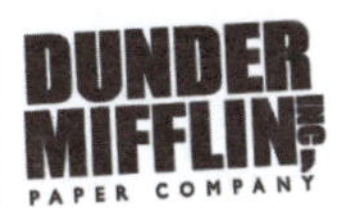

Week of:

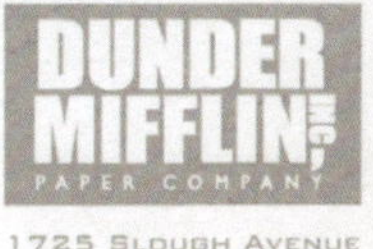

1725 Slough Avenue
Scranton, PA 18505

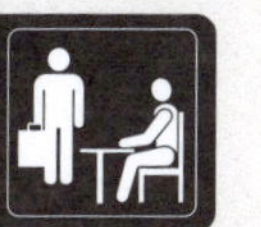

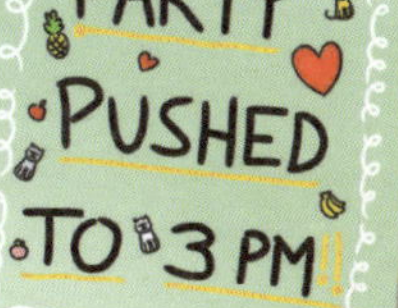

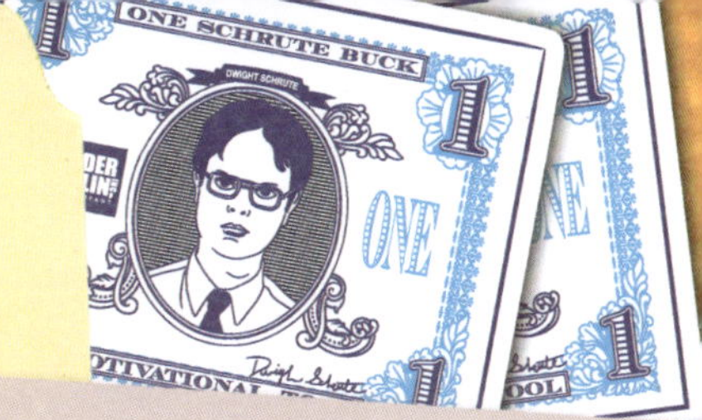

WEEKLY PLAN

NOTES

TOP PRIORITIES

MONDAY	TUESDAY
WEDNESDAY	THURSDAY
FRIDAY	SATURDAY
	SUNDAY

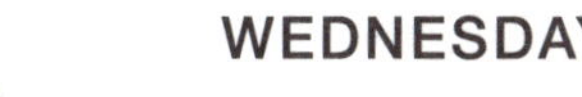

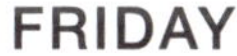

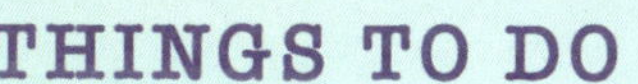

BEFORE I DO ANYTHING I ASK MYSELF, 'WOULD AN IDIOT DO THAT?' AND IF THE ANSWER IS YES, I DO NOT DO THAT THING.

THINGS TO DO

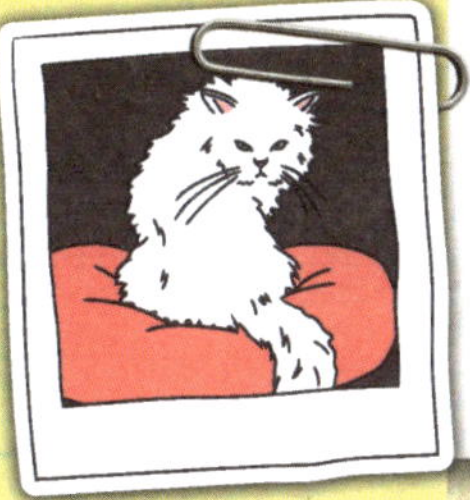

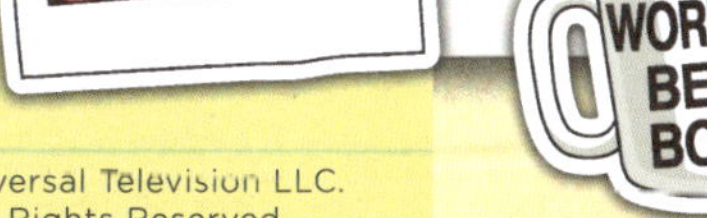

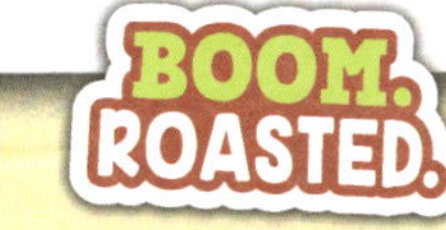

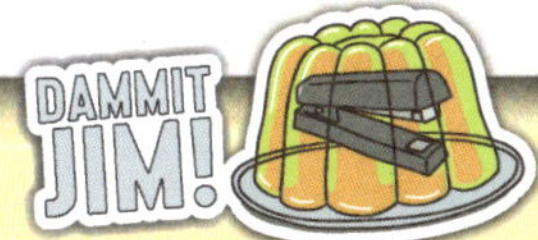

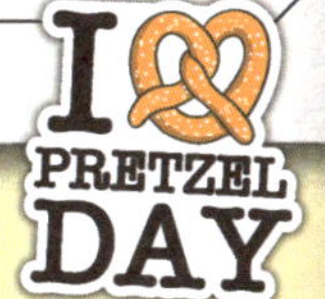

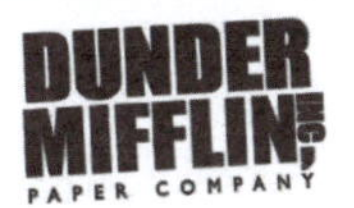

Week of:

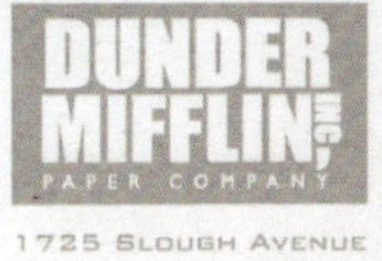

1725 Slough Avenue
Scranton, PA 18505

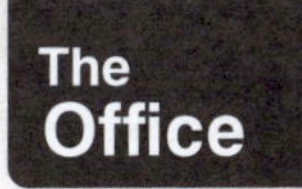

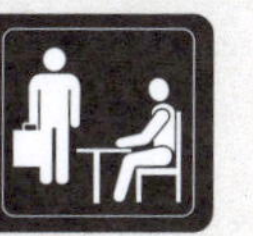

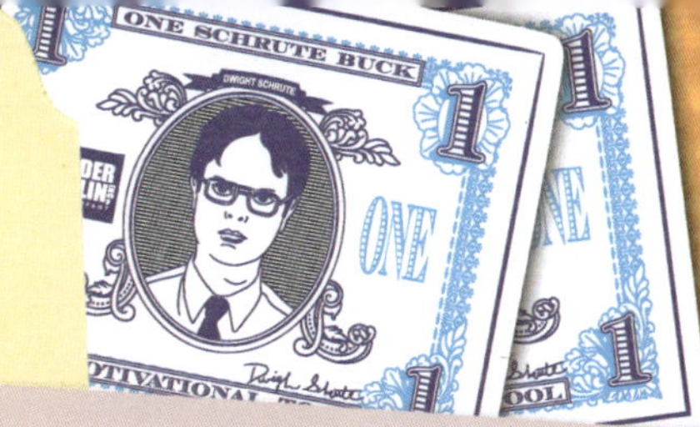

WEEKLY PLAN

NOTES

MONDAY	TUESDAY
WEDNESDAY	THURSDAY
FRIDAY	SATURDAY
	SUNDAY

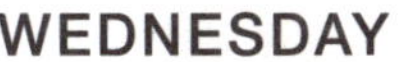

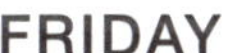

TOP PRIORITIES

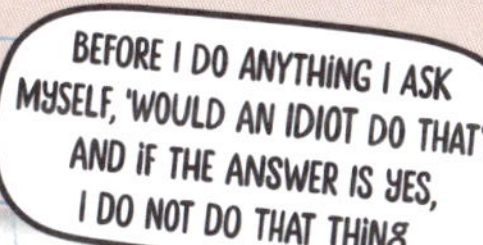

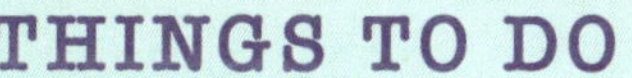

BEFORE I DO ANYTHING I ASK MYSELF, 'WOULD AN IDIOT DO THAT?' AND IF THE ANSWER IS YES, I DO NOT DO THAT THING.

THINGS TO DO

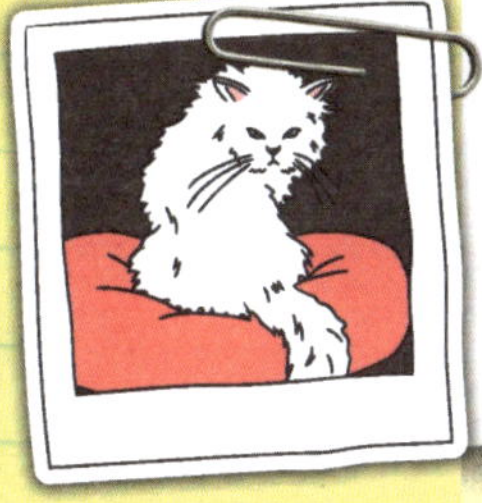

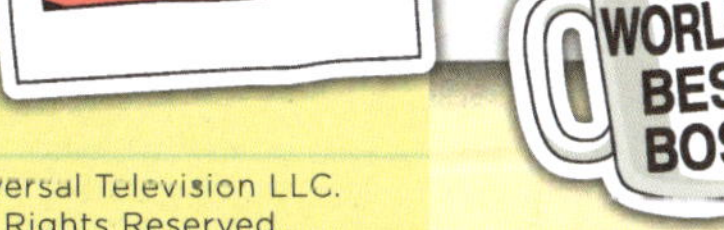

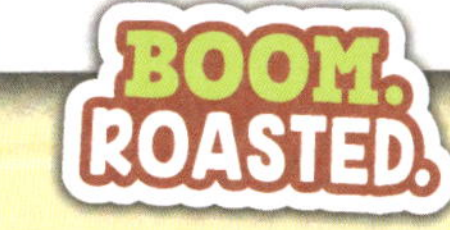

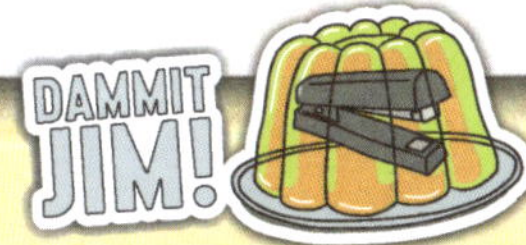

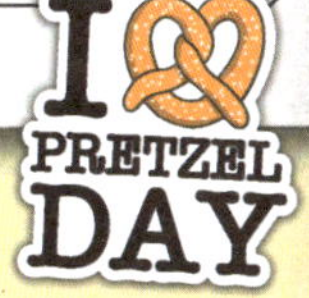

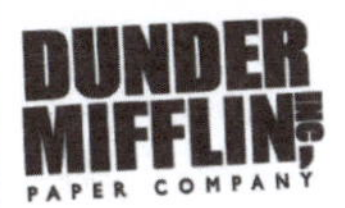

Week of:

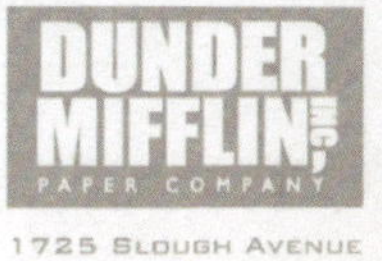

1725 Slough Avenue
Scranton, PA 18505

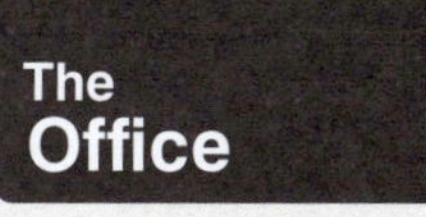

WEEKLY PLAN

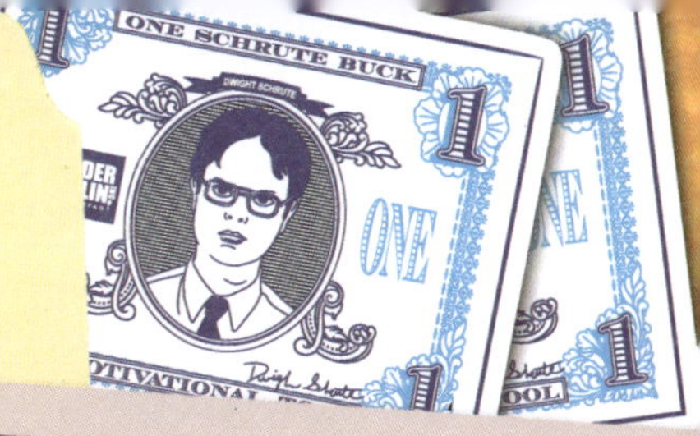

NOTES

TOP PRIORITIES

MONDAY	TUESDAY
WEDNESDAY	THURSDAY
FRIDAY	SATURDAY
	SUNDAY

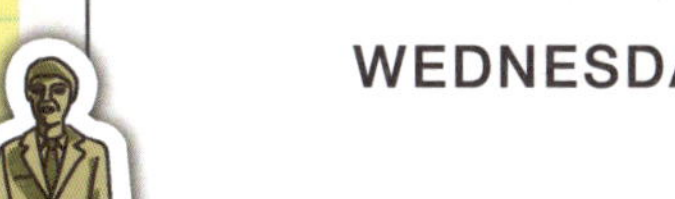

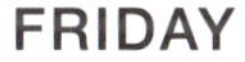

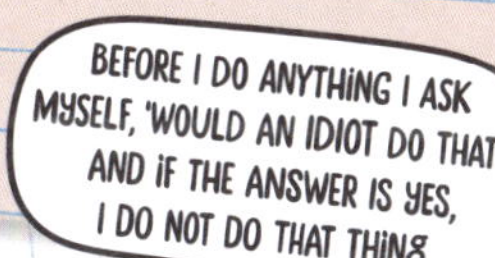

THINGS TO DO

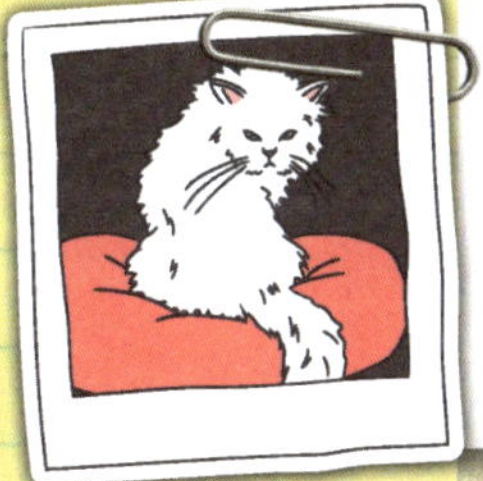

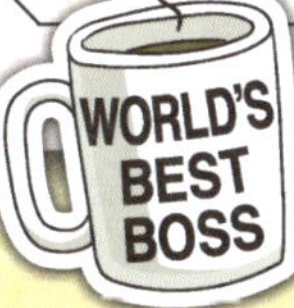

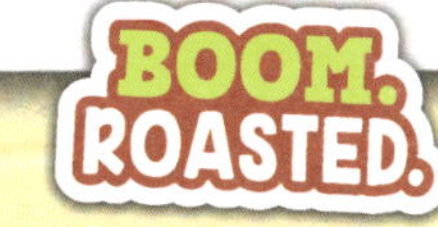

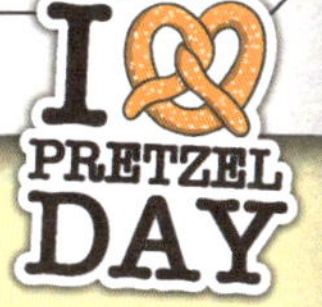

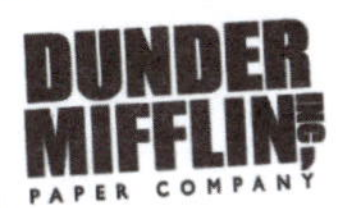

Week of:

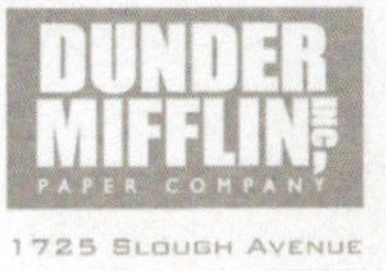

1725 Slough Avenue
Scranton, PA 18505

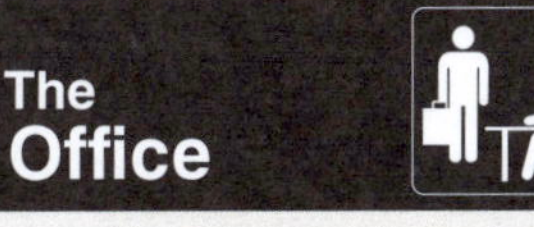

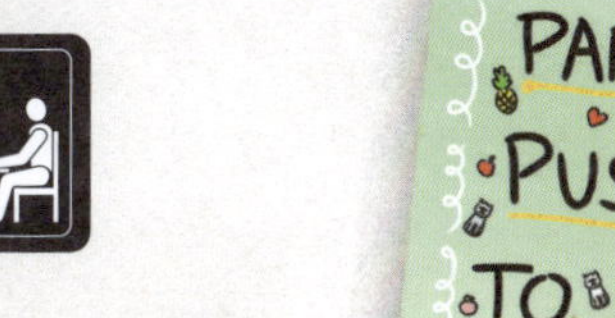

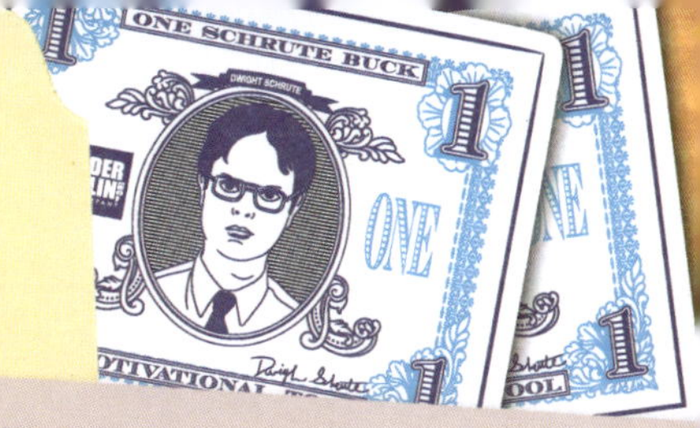

WEEKLY PLAN

NOTES

MONDAY	TUESDAY
WEDNESDAY	THURSDAY
FRIDAY	SATURDAY
	SUNDAY

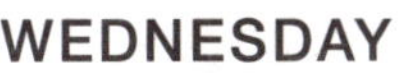

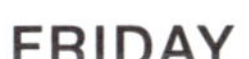

TOP PRIORITIES

BEFORE I DO ANYTHING I ASK MYSELF, 'WOULD AN IDIOT DO THAT?' AND IF THE ANSWER IS YES, I DO NOT DO THAT THING.

THINGS TO DO

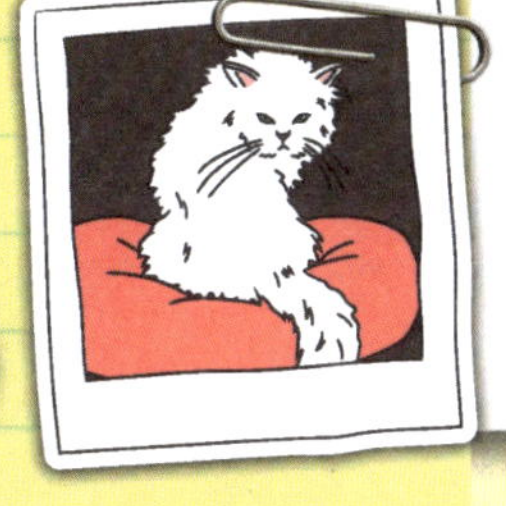

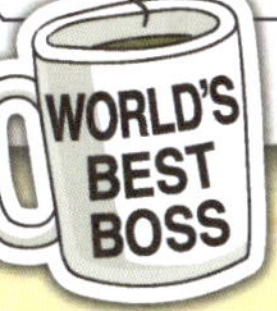

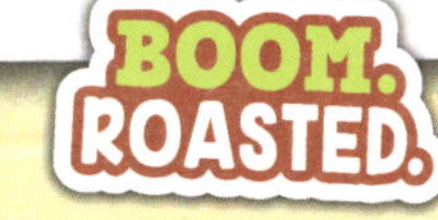

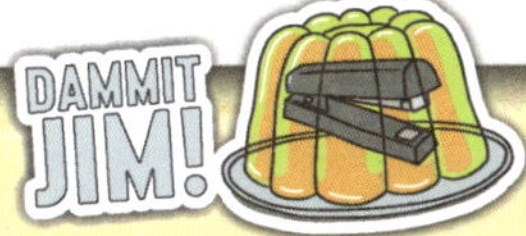

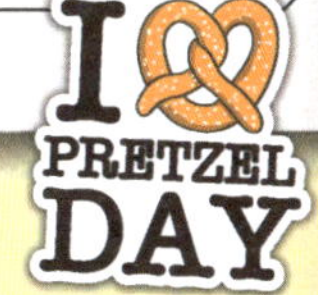

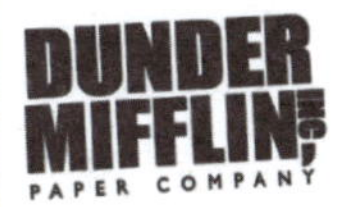

Week of:

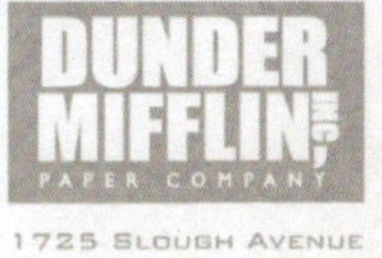

1725 Slough Avenue
Scranton, PA 18505

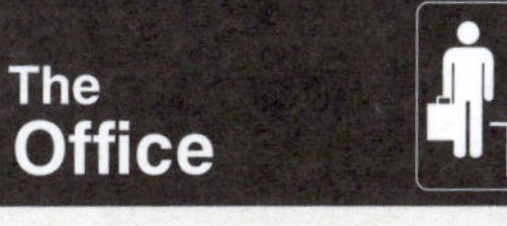

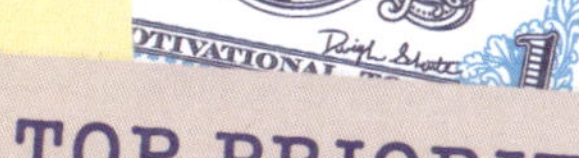

WEEKLY PLAN

NOTES

MONDAY	TUESDAY
WEDNESDAY	THURSDAY
FRIDAY	SATURDAY
	SUNDAY

TOP PRIORITIES

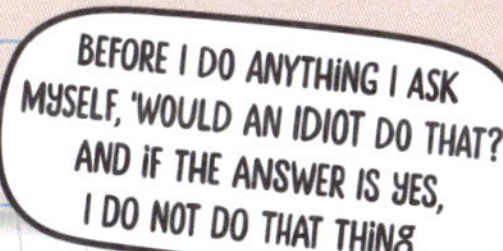

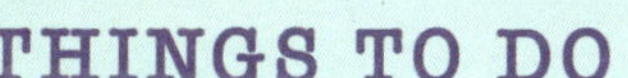

THINGS TO DO

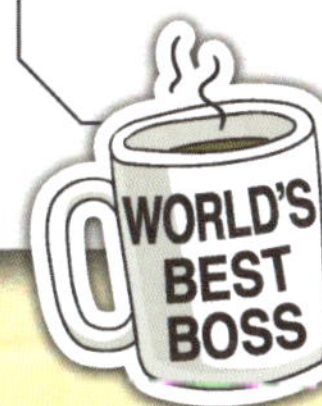
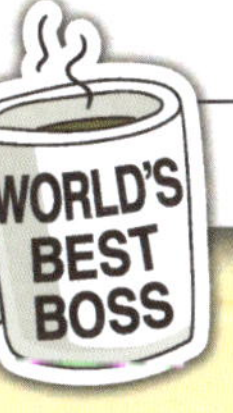

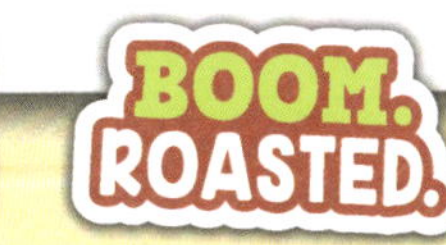

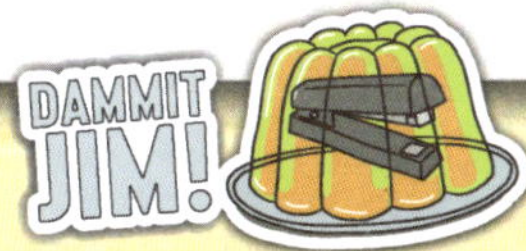

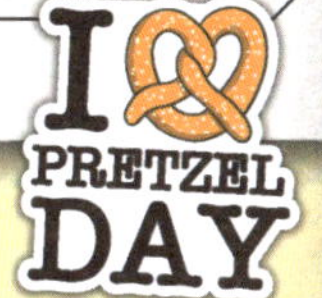

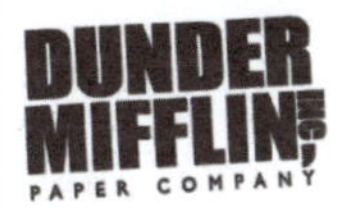

Week of:

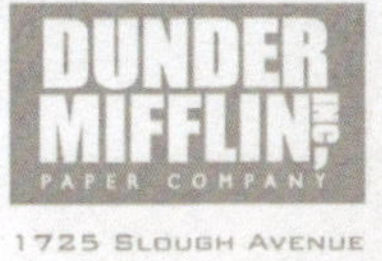

1725 Slough Avenue
Scranton, PA 18505

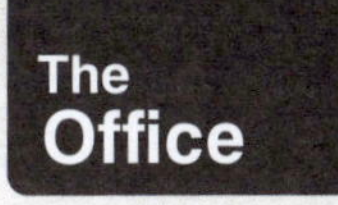

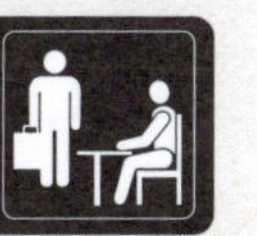

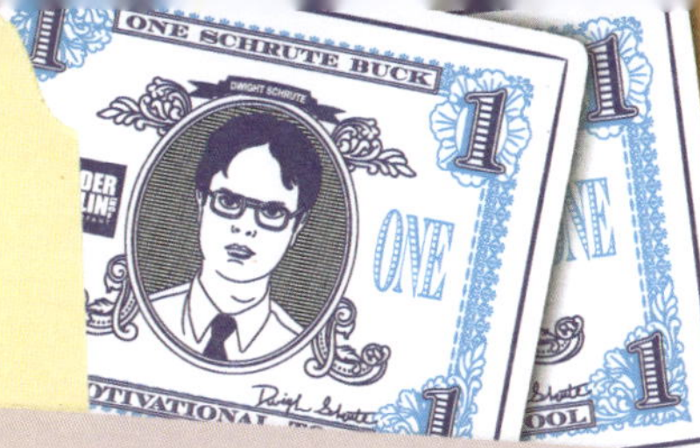

WEEKLY PLAN

NOTES

MONDAY	TUESDAY
WEDNESDAY	THURSDAY
FRIDAY	SATURDAY
	SUNDAY

TOP PRIORITIES

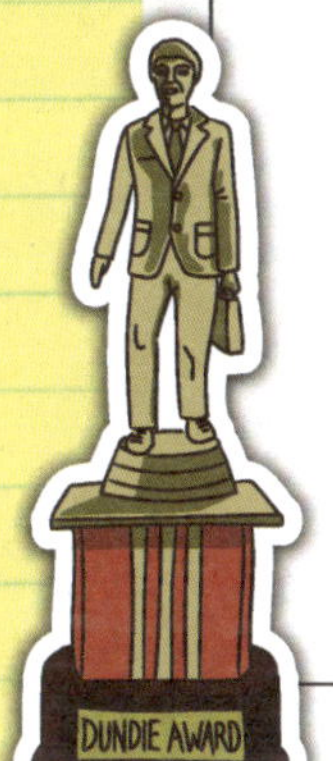

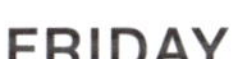

BEFORE I DO ANYTHING I ASK MYSELF, 'WOULD AN IDIOT DO THAT?' AND IF THE ANSWER IS YES, I DO NOT DO THAT THING.

THINGS TO DO

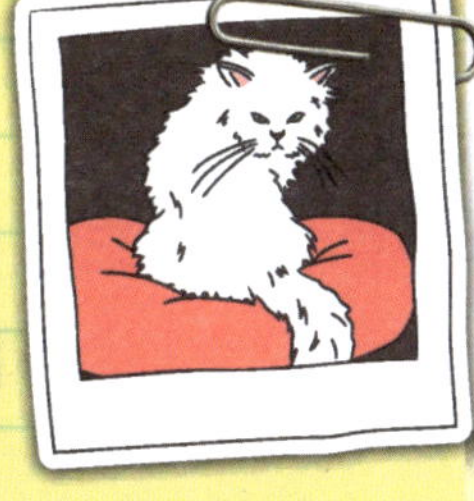

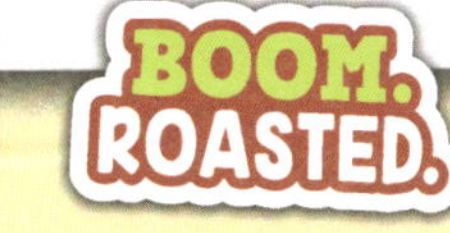

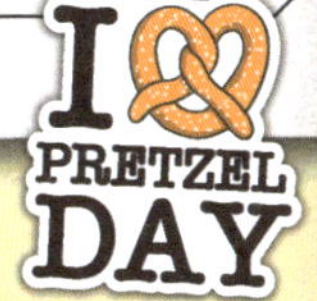

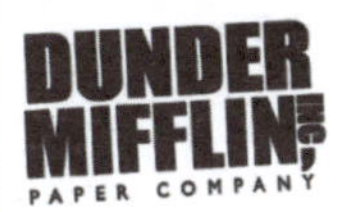

Week of:

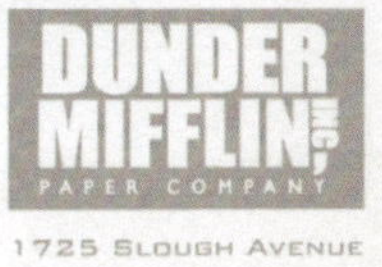

1725 SLOUGH AVENUE
SCRANTON, PA 18505

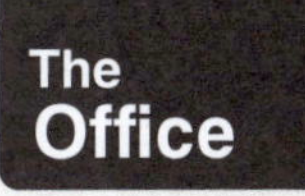

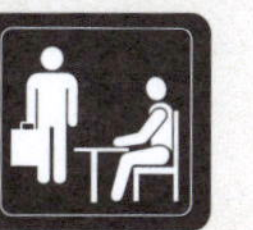

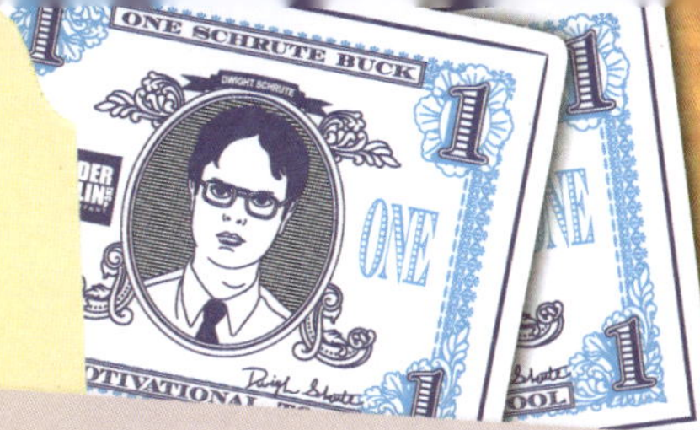

WEEKLY PLAN

NOTES

MONDAY	TUESDAY
WEDNESDAY	THURSDAY
FRIDAY	SATURDAY
	SUNDAY

TOP PRIORITIES

BEFORE I DO ANYTHING I ASK MYSELF, 'WOULD AN IDIOT DO THAT?' AND IF THE ANSWER IS YES, I DO NOT DO THAT THING.

DUNDIE AWARD

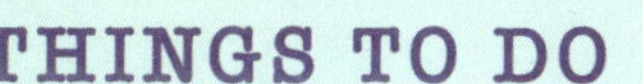

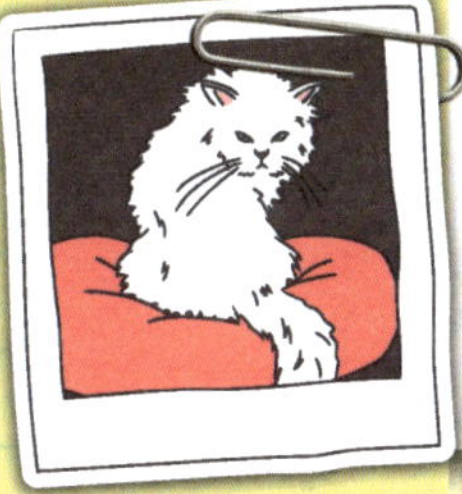

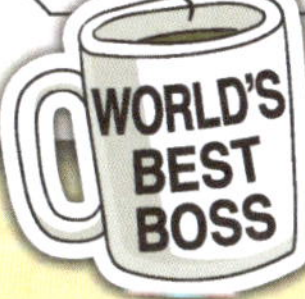

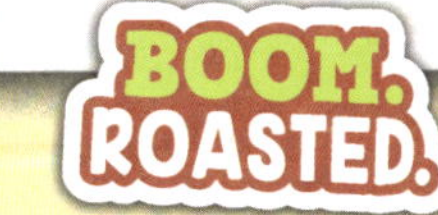

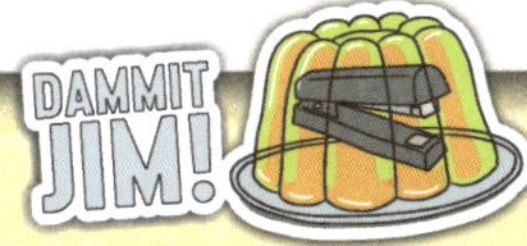

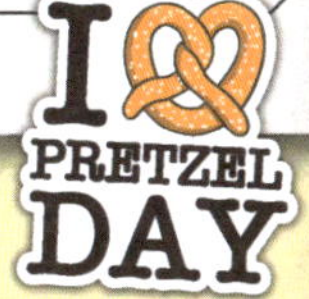

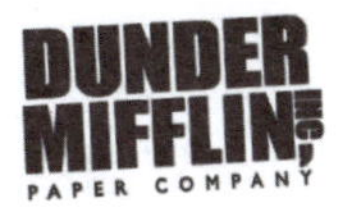

Week of:

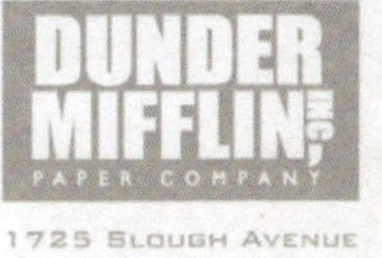

1725 Slough Avenue
Scranton, PA 18505

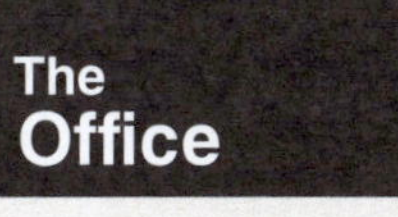

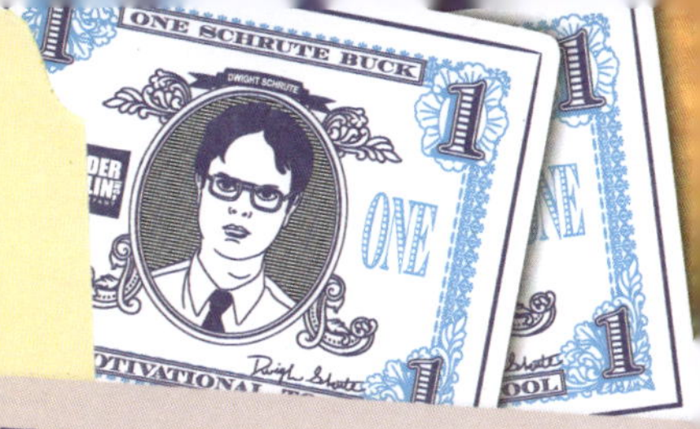

WEEKLY PLAN

NOTES

MONDAY	TUESDAY
WEDNESDAY	THURSDAY
FRIDAY	SATURDAY
	SUNDAY

TOP PRIORITIES

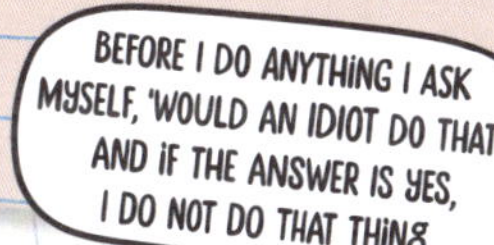

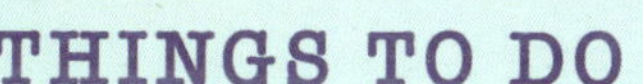

THINGS TO DO

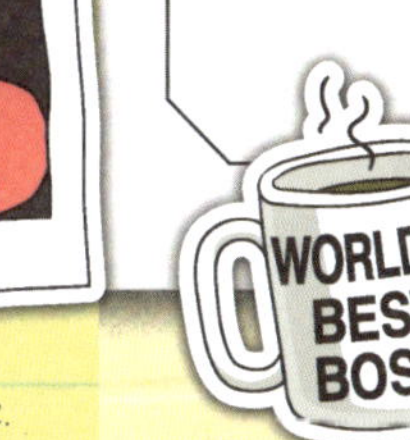

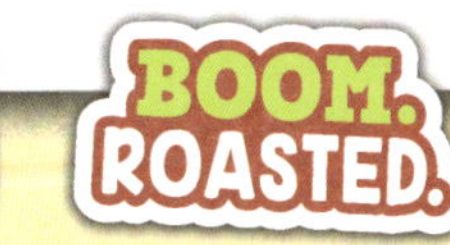

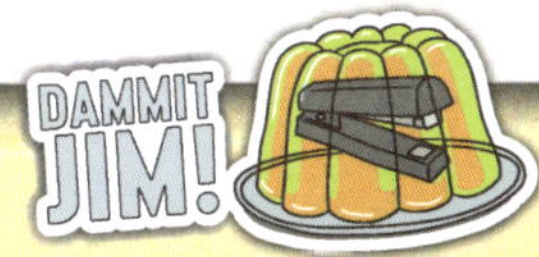

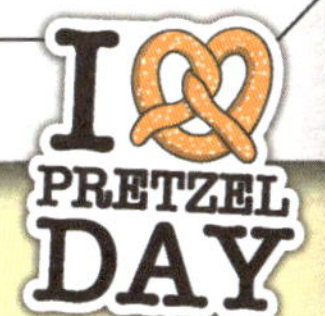

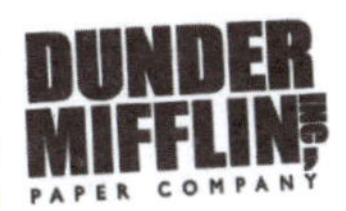

Week of:

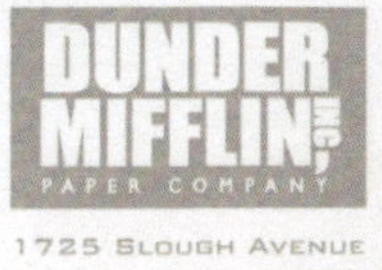

1725 Slough Avenue
Scranton, PA 18505

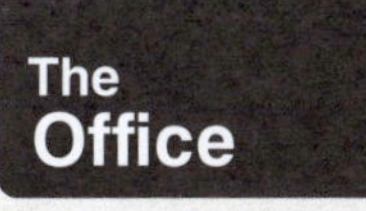

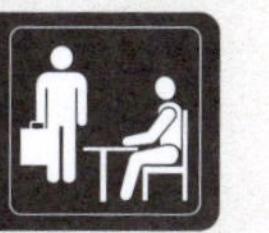

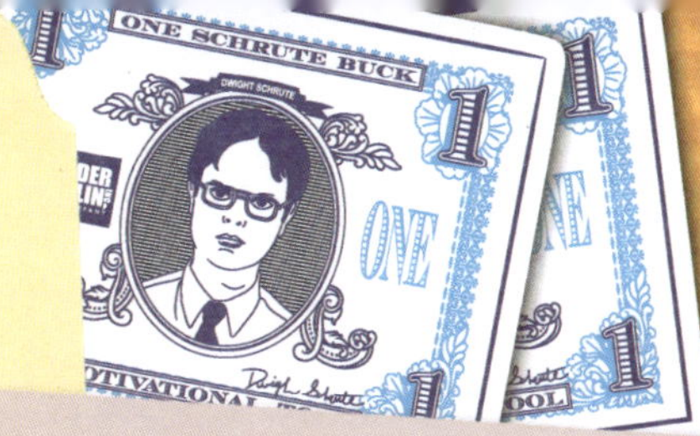

WEEKLY PLAN

NOTES

<table>
<tr><td>MONDAY</td><td>TUESDAY</td></tr>
<tr><td>WEDNESDAY</td><td>THURSDAY</td></tr>
<tr><td rowspan="2">FRIDAY</td><td>SATURDAY</td></tr>
<tr><td>SUNDAY</td></tr>
</table>

TOP PRIORITIES

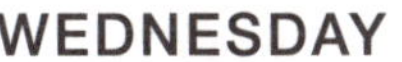

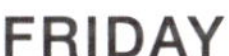

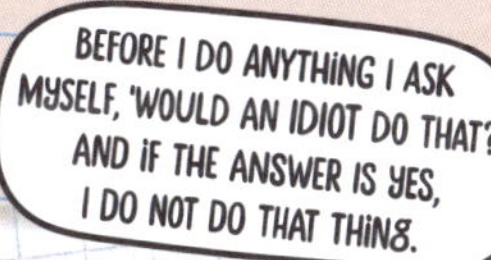

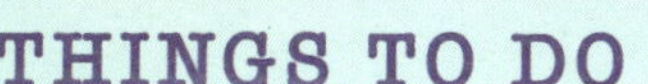

THINGS TO DO

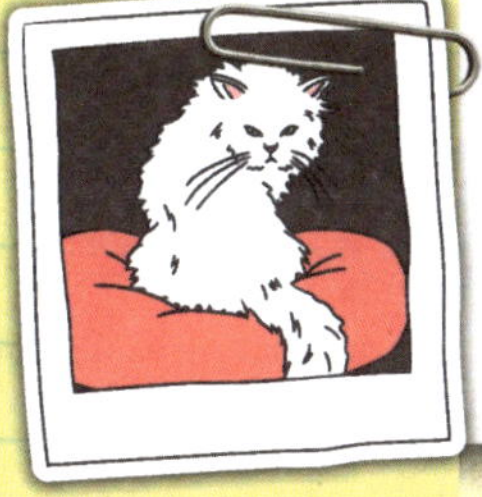

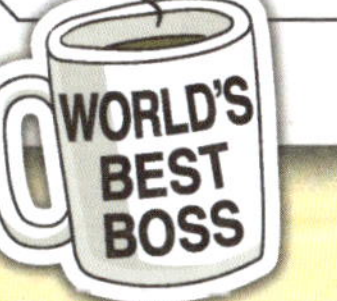

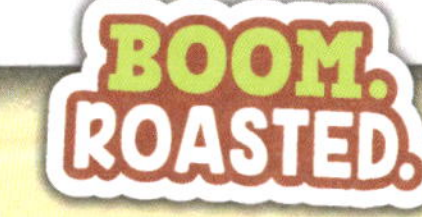

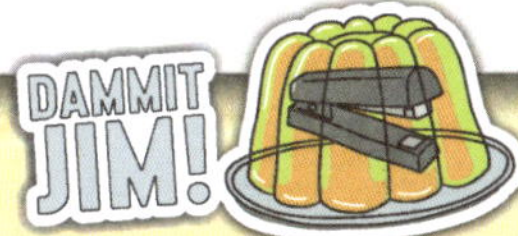

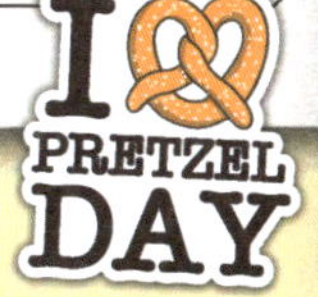

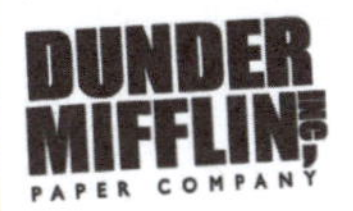

Week of:

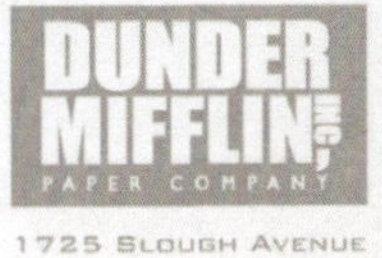

1725 Slough Avenue
Scranton, PA 18505

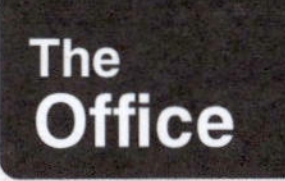

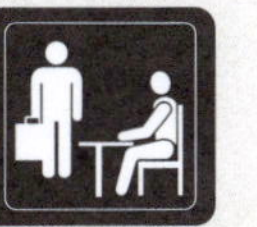

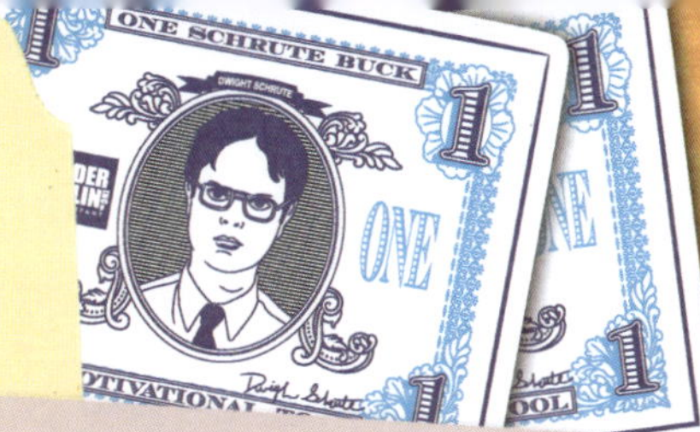

WEEKLY PLAN

NOTES

MONDAY	TUESDAY
WEDNESDAY	THURSDAY
FRIDAY	SATURDAY
	SUNDAY

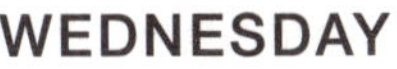

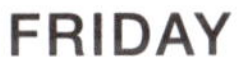

TOP PRIORITIES

BEFORE I DO ANYTHING I ASK MYSELF, 'WOULD AN IDIOT DO THAT?' AND IF THE ANSWER IS YES, I DO NOT DO THAT THING.

THINGS TO DO

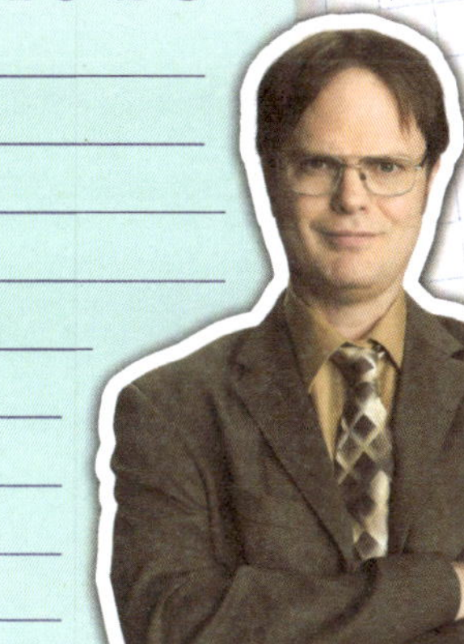

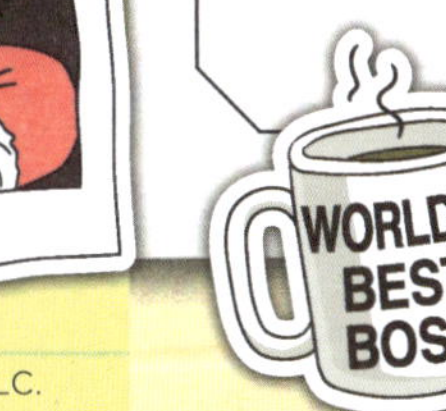

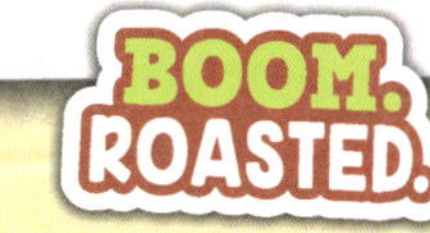

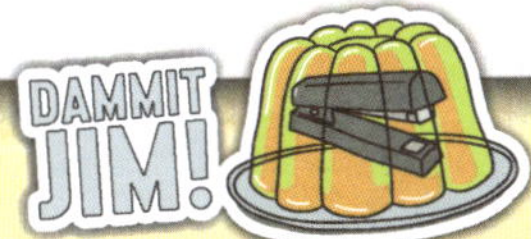

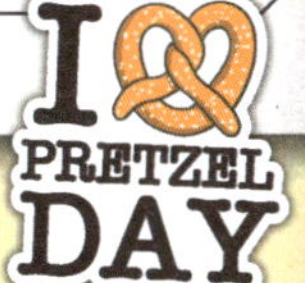

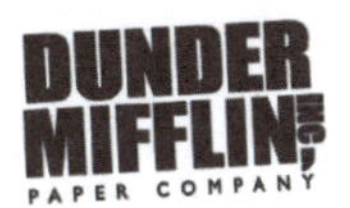

Week of:

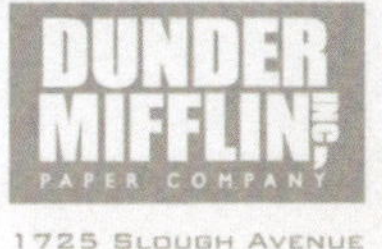

1725 Slough Avenue
Scranton, PA 18505

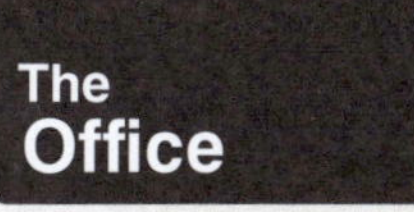

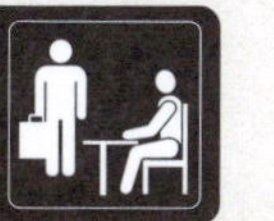

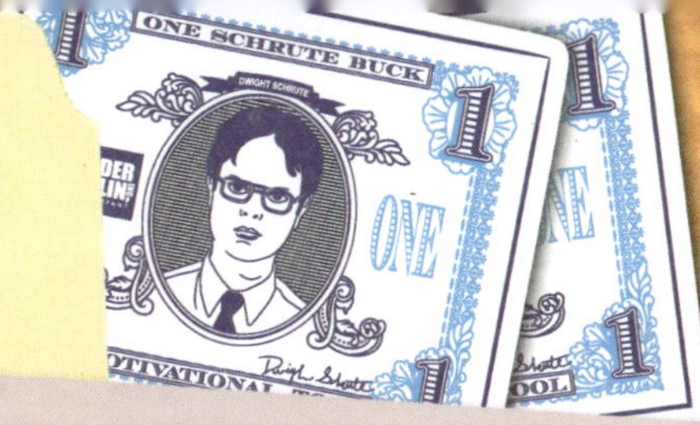

WEEKLY PLAN

NOTES

MONDAY	TUESDAY
WEDNESDAY	THURSDAY
FRIDAY	SATURDAY
	SUNDAY

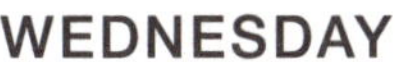

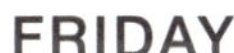

TOP PRIORITIES

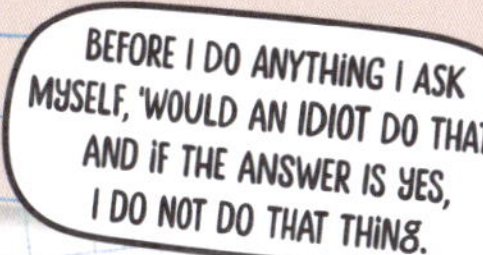

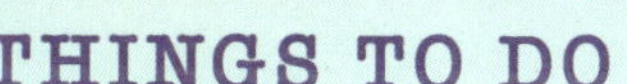

THINGS TO DO

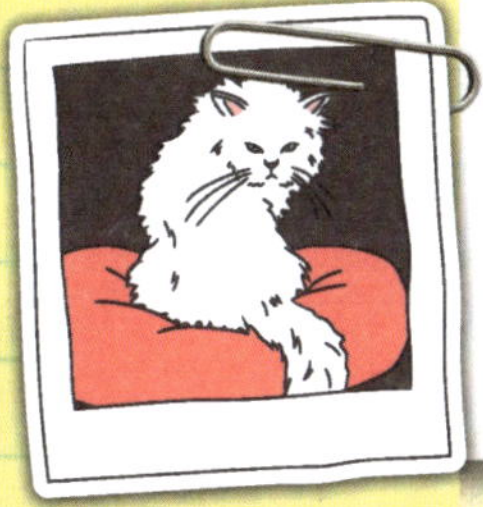

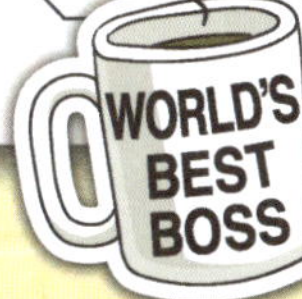

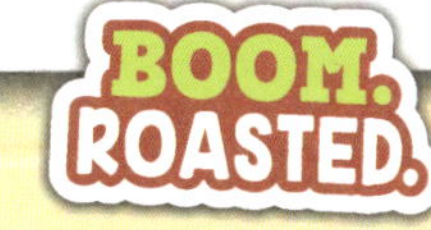

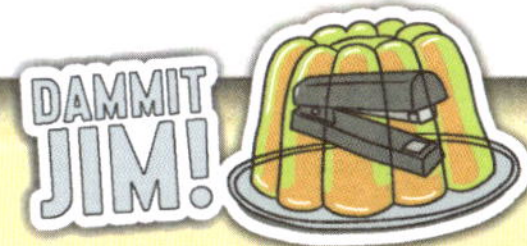

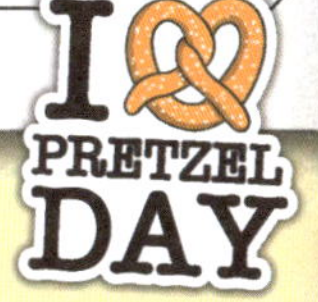

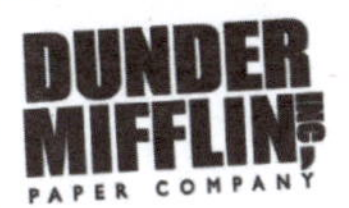

Week of:

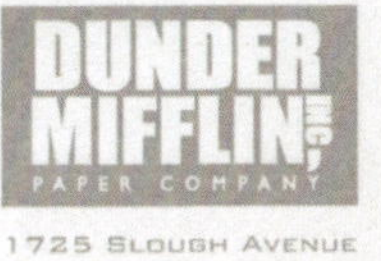

1725 Slough Avenue
Scranton, PA 18505

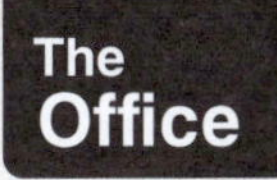

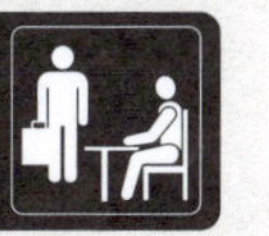

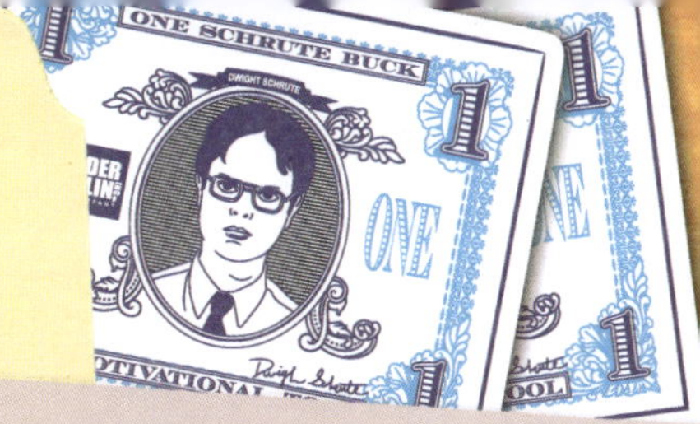

WEEKLY PLAN

NOTES

MONDAY	TUESDAY
WEDNESDAY	THURSDAY
FRIDAY	SATURDAY
	SUNDAY

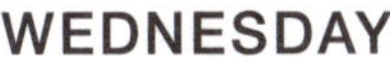

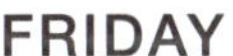

TOP PRIORITIES

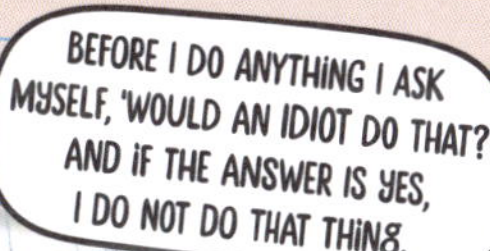

BEFORE I DO ANYTHING I ASK MYSELF, 'WOULD AN IDIOT DO THAT?' AND IF THE ANSWER IS YES, I DO NOT DO THAT THING.

THINGS TO DO

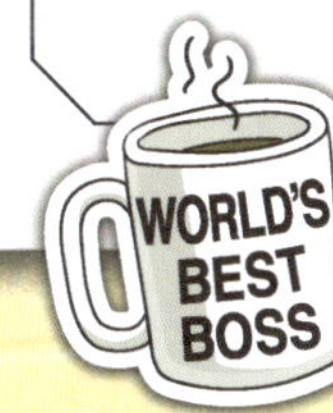

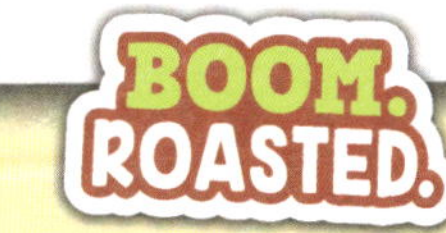

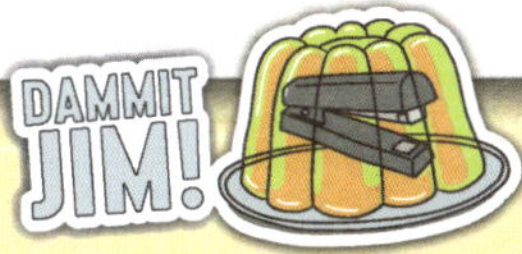

I PRETZEL DAY

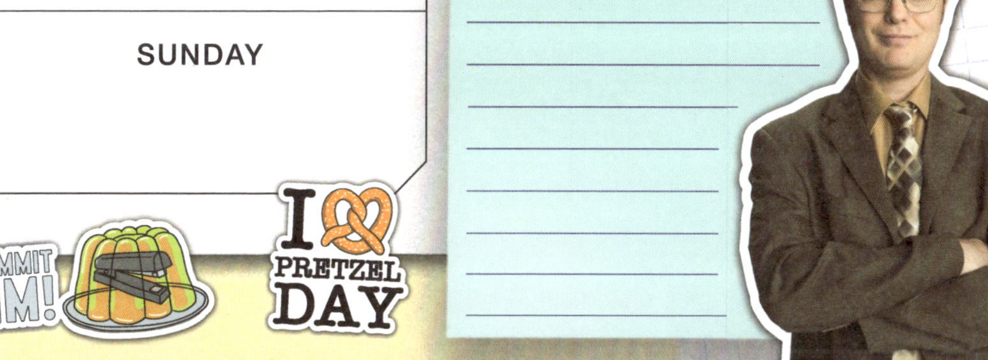

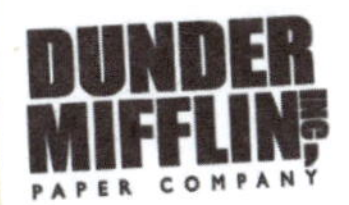

Week of:

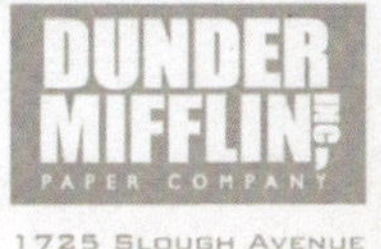

1725 Slough Avenue
Scranton, PA 18505

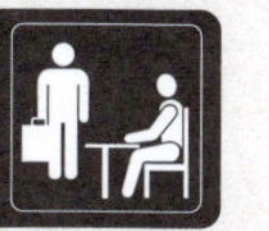

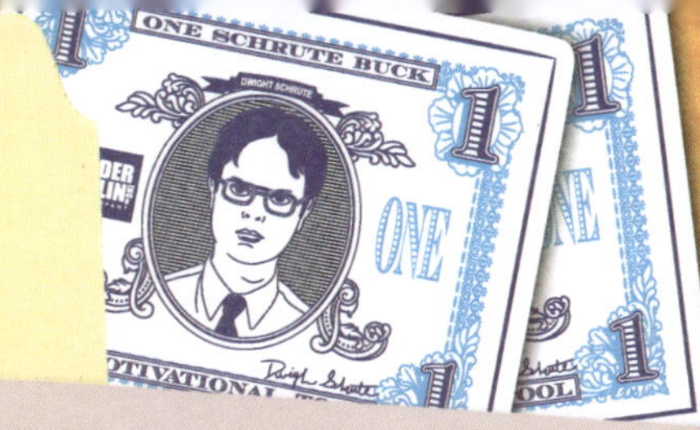

WEEKLY PLAN

NOTES

MONDAY	TUESDAY
WEDNESDAY	**THURSDAY**
FRIDAY	**SATURDAY**
	SUNDAY

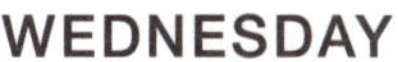

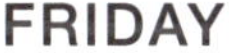

TOP PRIORITIES

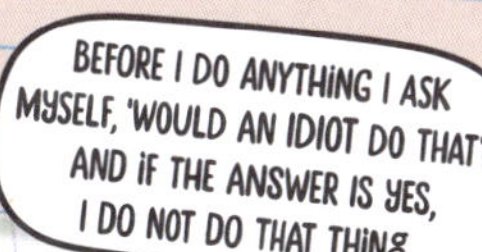

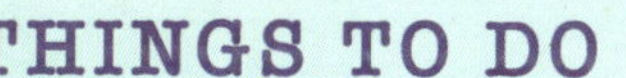

BEFORE I DO ANYTHING I ASK MYSELF, 'WOULD AN IDIOT DO THAT?' AND IF THE ANSWER IS YES, I DO NOT DO THAT THING.

THINGS TO DO

DUNDIE AWARD

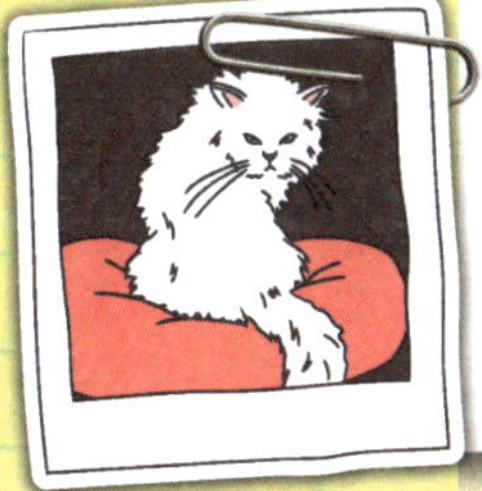

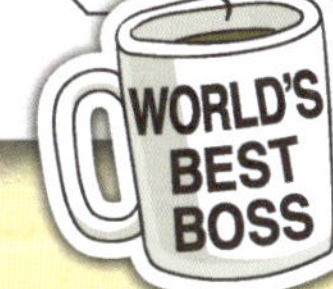

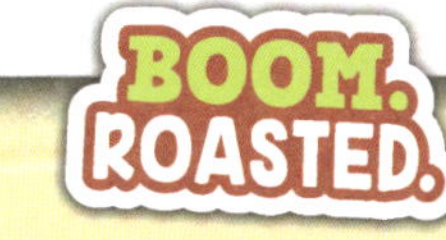

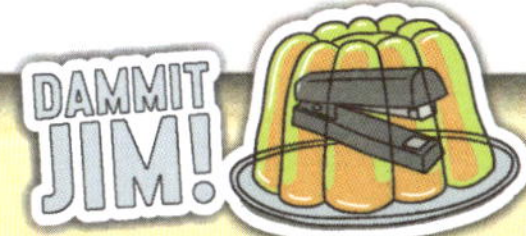

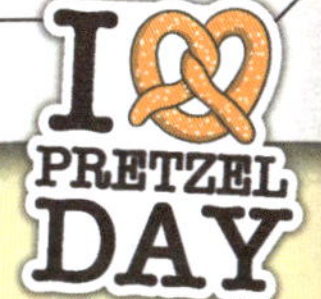

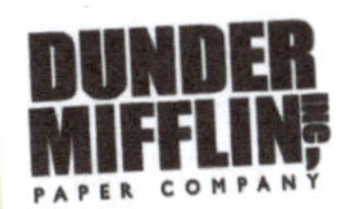

Week of:

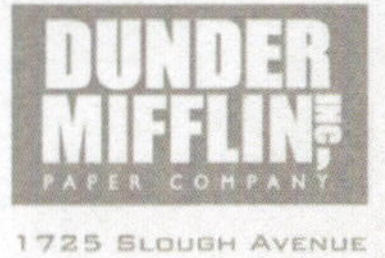

1725 Slough Avenue
Scranton, PA 18505

The Office

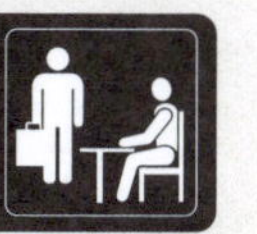

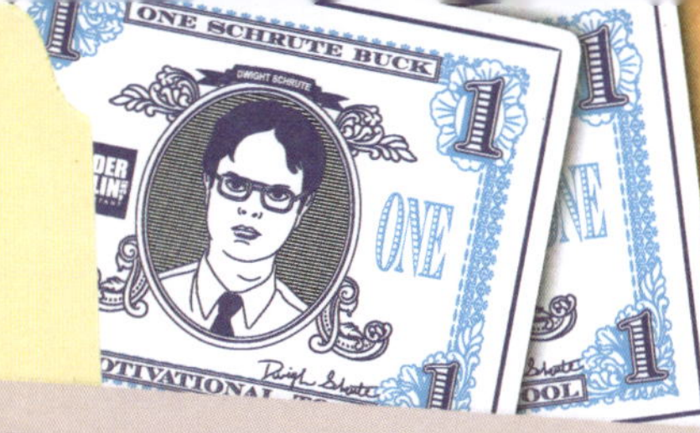

WEEKLY PLAN

NOTES

MONDAY	TUESDAY
WEDNESDAY	THURSDAY
FRIDAY	SATURDAY
	SUNDAY

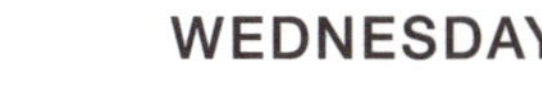

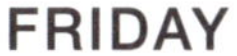

TOP PRIORITIES

BEFORE I DO ANYTHING I ASK MYSELF, 'WOULD AN IDIOT DO THAT?' AND IF THE ANSWER IS YES, I DO NOT DO THAT THING.

DUNDIE AWARD

THINGS TO DO

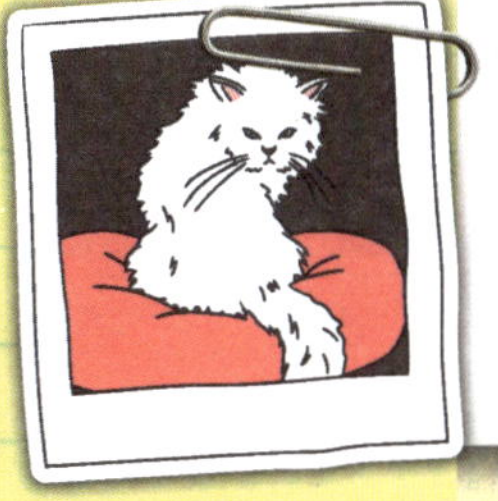

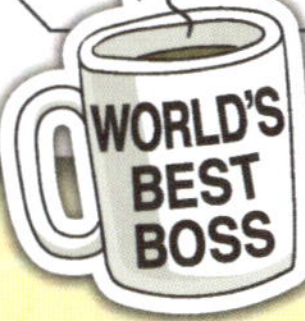

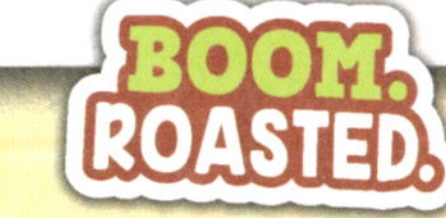

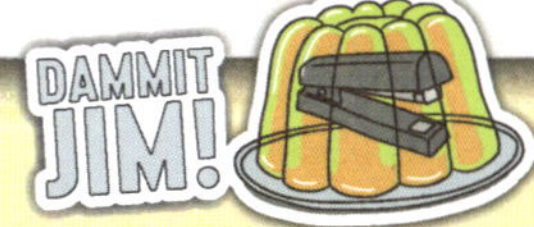

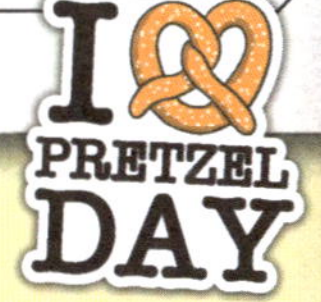